Secret Box Books #3

P9-DML-360

DISCARDED

THE
SECRET
FIRE

THE SECRET FIRE

DISCARDED

WHITAKER RINGWALD

KATHERINE TEGEN BOOKS
An Imprint of HarperCollins Publishers

Katherine Tegen Books is an imprint of HarperCollins Publishers.

The Secret Fire
Copyright © 2016 by HarperCollins
All rights reserved. Printed in the United States of America.
No part of this book may be used or reproduced in any manner
whatsoever without written permission except in the case of brief
quotations embodied in critical articles and reviews. For information
address HarperCollins Children's Books,
a division of HarperCollins Publishers, 195 Broadway,
New York, NY 10007.
www.harpercollinschildrens.com

Library of Congress Control Number: 2016930033
ISBN 978-0-06-221620-5

Typography by Carla Weise
16 17 18 19 20   CG/RRDH   10 9 8 7 6 5 4 3 2 1
❖
First Edition

The most powerful weapon on earth is the human soul on fire.
—Ferdinand Foch

1
JAX

I've always wanted to ride in a limousine. Movie stars get to ride in them all the time. And high school kids rent them for prom. This was a pretty nice one. It had a row of black leather seats that stretched along the windows and wrapped around the back end like the letter *J*. There was a minibar with crystal glasses and a refrigerator. Last year, our neighbors rented a limo for their daughter and she and her friends drove down our road with their heads sticking out the sunroof. They looked like they were having fun. I wanted to do that. I wanted to stick out my head.

But then I'd crawl right out onto the roof and

make my escape, because this limo ride was the opposite of fun.

I'd been hurrying down the steps of the Museum of Fine Arts in Boston, running as fast as I could because I was supposed to meet my cousins and this new friend of ours named Pyrrha. I'd just finished deactivating the museum's security system so that my cousins could steal an urn. We were supposed to meet at Tyler's car. It's not like I do that sort of thing every day so I was pretty nervous. I kept looking over my shoulder to make sure no guards were following me. And I didn't hear any police sirens so that was a good sign. As soon as I got to the car, I was going to check the phone to see if anyone had sent any texts. Ethan gave me his phone to borrow, so I'd have a way to communicate during our heist. But when I neared the end of the steps, there was this crazy man standing there. "Hello, Jacqueline," he said.

I skidded to a stop. If he'd been a total stranger, I would have wondered why, on such a hot day, he was wearing a long black coat. But he wasn't a stranger. His name was Ricardo. And I knew why his hand was in his pocket. He was hiding a weapon. Not a gun. Something way worse.

We stared at each other. His eyes were dark and empty. I don't know how to explain it but it was like looking into a robot's eyes. There was no twinkle, no rage—nothing. And he barely blinked. I was trying to decide if I should start running again, when a limousine pulled up to the curb behind him. "Come with me or you know what will happen," he told me, his expression dead calm.

I looked around for Ethan, Tyler, and Pyrrha. They weren't standing by our car. They weren't hurrying down the steps. That meant they were still inside the museum, still trying to steal the urn. And if this guy found out about the urn, we'd be in huge trouble.

He turned away for a moment, to open the limo's back door. That gave me just enough time to silence Ethan's phone and tuck it beneath my T-shirt, into the waistband of my shorts. I'd borrowed Ethan's phone because I didn't have one of my own, which is a sore spot with me. What twelve-year-old doesn't have a phone? Seriously!

Ricardo motioned for me to get into the limo.

"What if I don't go?" I threatened. "What if I start screaming for help?"

"Why would you do such a useless thing?" He

patted his pocket. "You know what will happen."

I shot darts at him with my glare. I knew, without a doubt, that another urn was tucked inside his pocket. Even though I'd never seen this particular urn in person, I'd heard all about it. It was called the urn of Faith, and if Ricardo opened it, a magical windstorm would burst out. The wind would be so strong it would break tree branches and knock people over. Cyclists would fly off their bikes, cars would crash, windows would break. Then the magic would reach out like a million cold fingers and yank faith from the souls of anyone who happened to be standing in its path.

Losing faith might not sound like a big deal. There are times when we all give up, because we're disappointed, or because something terrible happened. We might stop believing in ourselves or in a higher power. But that's only a percentage of the faith we carry around with us every single day. Even if we feel that we have nothing left, our faith can be reignited. It can grow. It's like the seasons, or like the tide, coming and going, moving in and out. But the urn takes every single drop. It sucks the soul totally dry. There's nothing to ignite. Nothing to water or fertilize. And once the urn has done its damage, its victims search desperately for something to believe in. Anything. Anyone.

They turn to Ricardo. And they put their faith in him. They become his followers. His servants.

I wasn't going to let that happen to me, or to Ethan or Tyler. Or our new friend, Pyrrha. Or to anyone who had the bad luck to be in the wrong place at the wrong time.

So I got into the limo. Never, never, never get into a car with a stranger, Mom always said. But these circumstances were different. I knew this guy, sorta. And besides, what else could I do? We hadn't come up with a backup plan.

Ricardo got in and sat in the seat across from me. He closed the door, then the limo started to move. I took a sharp breath. Had I made the wrong decision?

I couldn't see the driver because of a tinted plate of glass that separated the front seat from the back of the limo. To my surprise, we didn't drive very far. In fact, we drove into the art museum's parking lot and sat, idling. I narrowed my eyes. What was he waiting for? Was he going to try to capture my cousins, too? I had to warn them. I pressed my fingers against the window. Ethan and Tyler still hadn't come out of the museum. Nor had Pyrrha. I glanced at Ricardo's pocket.

As far as I knew, there were three magical urns—the urn of Faith, the urn of Love, and the urn of Hope. I'd only seen the urn of Hope. I'd carried it around. I'd even slept with it in my hotel bed. For a while, I'd been its protector. I remember how warm it had felt in my hands, like a living creature. I'd been able to sense when it was nearby. I could hear it calling me. But as I sat in the limo, I didn't sense the urn of Faith. That didn't surprise me. I'd never acted as its protector so I guess we had no bond. But as Ricardo settled into his seat, his coat pocket suddenly looked flat. Too flat to be holding anything. "Wait a minute," I said. "Let me see the urn."

Ricardo took off his fedora and set it on his lap. He tucked his long black hair behind his ears, then looked at me with a blank expression. "How can I show it to you? It is not here."

"What?" I cried.

"Did you think I carried it with me at all times?" He shook his head with disgust. "A weapon of such magnificence should always be kept in a safe place. And brought out only when needed."

He'd tricked me. I felt so stupid. I should have

demanded to see it when we were on the museum steps. I punched the door button. The window buttons. Nothing opened. Did this limo have child-protection locks? I always hated those things! I pounded my feet on the floor, yelling at the driver. "Hey! There's a kidnapped girl back here!" I pounded my fists on the windows. "Help! Help!" People walked down the sidewalk but no one turned and looked at the limo. Had it been sound-proofed? I thought about the phone, still hidden in my waistband. It was too risky. If Ricardo saw it, he'd take it away. That phone might be my best chance for escape.

Why had I let him trick me? I was furious!

"Calm down," he told me, his voice as cold as steel. His fingers twitched, as if there was elec-tricity running through them. He pulled a phone from the inner pocket of his coat and made a call. I stopped thrashing and watched, gripping the edge of my seat. "Hello, Tyler Hoche. Are you ready to turn over the urn of Hope?" He'd called my cousin.

"Don't give it to him!" I shouted.

Even though the phone was pressed to Ricar-do's ear, I could hear Tyler's muffled voice call my name.

7

"That is correct," Ricardo replied. "Jacqueline is with me. I will keep her unless you are willing to make a trade."

Then a girl's voice shot out of the speaker so loud, Ricardo winced. "Do not hurt her! Do you hear me, Father? Do not injure Jacqueline Malone."

Father?

For a moment, Ricardo's expression softened. It was as if his icy mask had melted away, revealing a real, living person. "Pyrrha? Is that you? What are you doing in this world? You are forbidden to be here. You are breaking Zeus's law. You are in danger." He actually sounded concerned. This monster who had unleashed the urn of Faith in two different banks and had hurt dozens of people actually *cared* about someone?

But wait a minute. Ricardo was Pyrrha's father? I was so shocked, I went kinda numb. That meant that he was also from the Realm of the Gods. He was *immortal*. My brain flooded with questions, but I forced myself to sit quietly and listen.

On the other end of the call, Pyrrha pleaded with her father to come home. To help her destroy the urns once and for all. "Please, Father, stop this madness. Zeus has Hope and—"

His eyes turned cold once again. "You returned Hope?" He held the phone closer.

I could no longer hear Pyrrha. But at that moment, Ricardo's eyes flashed as red as a flame. "The gods never forgive," he hissed. "They cannot be trusted. Why would I go back to a world where I have no power, when this world offers me wealth and glory beyond measure? Come to me, my darling daughter, and together, we will rebuild the world of the gods in our own image. Together, we shall rule this world."

Rebuild the world of the gods? I felt like I was watching a movie. The guy was nuts!

There was another long pause as he listened to his daughter. Then his gaze rested on my sneakers. "Give up your quest, Pyrrha, and she will not be hurt." He ended the call.

She will not be hurt. He was talking about *me*. I tried not to flinch. I tried to look brave.

We sat there for what seemed like forever. A few minutes ago I'd believed Ricardo was a maniac, but now I knew he was some kind of *immortal* maniac who wanted to *rule this world*. How could we possibly stop him? "You're wasting your time," I told him. I folded my arms so tightly, they started to ache. "Pyrrha will *never* help you. She knows the urns have to be destroyed. She'll *never* be on your side."

He said nothing. Then he rapped on the driver's window. The limo pulled out of the parking lot, then slowed again. Ricardo reached for the door. My heart skipped a beat. Was he going to let me out? I got ready to bolt.

But when the door opened, Pyrrha slipped into the backseat next to me.

"I will give up my quest, Father," she told him. "I will help you."

I couldn't believe it.

"Traitor," I said right to her face.

2
ETHAN

FACT: *A quest is a search or pursuit made in order to find or obtain something.*

In movies and books, the main character almost always goes on some sort of quest. I suppose that in those first stories, told by cavemen around the fire, the quest was to hunt and kill a great woolly mammoth. Later, the quest was to rescue a damsel in distress. In one of my favorite stories as a kid, the quest was to protect a giant peach from being destroyed by sharks and Cloud-Men.

But in this story, the one being told right now, the quest is for two brothers from Chatham, New Jersey, to save their cousin and the entire world from a madman.

Only this isn't a piece of fiction. This quest is real.

"Follow that car!" I hollered.

I couldn't believe those words had come from my mouth. That's one of those phrases you always hear in action films. If I were to star in a film, it would most likely be a documentary about how to check books out at the library, or a comedy about a shy kid who gets nosebleeds. I'm definitely not action-hero material. I can't even run a mile without starting to wheeze, thanks to my pollen allergy.

The car we needed to follow was a black limousine, and it was heading down the street with my cousin, Jax, held hostage in the backseat.

"Tyler!" I called. "Hurry up. Ricardo's getting away!"

Tyler looked a bit dazed. His hair was an uncombed mess, as usual, and his chin was covered in stubble. He didn't want to be here. But Jax and I had begged him to bring us to Boston. We'd needed him for practical reasons—he had a driver's license *and* a car. But we'd needed him for other reasons too. He was smart. He was strong. And he was just as involved in this mess as we were.

We'd kept the truth about this situation from our parents, and now that Jax was in danger, Tyler and I only had each other. I cringed. We didn't have a reputation for working well together.

This whole thing was supposed to be over. I'd wanted to spend the rest of the muggy summer with my feet in our backyard pool, sipping lemonade. Or riding my bike. Or reading. Or doing anything that would be considered sane, rational, and normal. Not worrying about dangerous Greek artifacts or a crazy guy who wanted to take over the world.

"Ricardo is Pyrrha's father?" Tyler mumbled.

We were standing in a parking lot, outside the Museum of Fine Arts in Boston. And if I looked as dazed as Tyler, I had good reason. We'd just stolen an urn from the museum's maintenance room. I don't know if this argument would stand up in court, but *technically* we hadn't stolen it. It was called the urn of Love and it had been hidden inside a small statue, which meant that while the statue was listed in the museum's directory, the urn wasn't.

The curators knew nothing about it.

The urn belonged to my great-aunt Juniper. She's the one who'd stuck it inside the statue for safekeeping. But Juniper was lying in a hospital bed, recovering from a stroke, so it had been up to us to get the urn back. Jax disabled the museum's security system. While Tyler and Pyrrha created a distraction, I went into the maintenance room, opened the statue, and took the urn. Then I managed to sneak it out of the museum. We were a success. No alarms rang, no security guards chased after us, and no police were waiting to arrest us.

Except our cousin, Jax, was supposed to meet us by the car and then we'd all go back home, and everything would be over.

"Tyler, you need to drive!" I cried. I yanked on his sleeve. "We need to follow them!"

"I can't believe he's her father."

"TYLER!"

He snapped out of it. He jumped into the driver's seat. I jumped into the passenger seat. We slammed the doors. I fastened my seat belt, then cradled the urn of Love between my palms. It radiated, like one of those hand warmers you put into your gloves when you go skiing. Sweat broke out on the back of my neck.

"Go!" I cried as the limousine turned a corner. Jax was disappearing before my eyes. Kidnapped by a lunatic. I felt totally helpless. "Drive!"

Tyler fumbled in his jeans. "Where's the key?"

"Are you serious?" My voice cracked.

"Oh, found it." He jammed the key into the ignition. The engine roared to life. As Tyler backed out of the parking space, he nearly hit a pair of tourists who'd been visiting the museum. Then he put the car into drive and started out of the parking lot. Something made a sputtering noise. The car jolted once, twice. We stopped moving.

"Drive!" I yelled again. "Go!" I was sounding like a broken record. With each second that passed, Jax was being taken farther and farther away. "Why aren't we moving?"

Tyler turned the key. Nothing happened. Then we both stared at the gas gauge.

Empty.

"No way!" Tyler pounded on the steering wheel.

"Empty? How can it be *empty*? Why didn't you fill the tank?" This was *his* fault. During this whole trip I'd been sitting in the backseat, navigating. I couldn't even see the gas gauge from the backseat. But he'd been looking right at it. He was to blame. *Someone* was to blame. Tears stung my eyes. How would we find Jax now?

"When, *exactly*, was I supposed to fill the tank?" he began his defense, his eyes narrowing with rage. "We were racing to get here, remember? We were trying to get the urn before Ricardo found us. I was driving as fast as I could. I wasn't thinking about gas!" He pounded the steering wheel again.

Tyler had a wicked temper. He mostly controlled it, but when it flared, it was fierce. He'd gotten in trouble a couple of times at school. He'd kicked over a desk. He'd thrown a wastebasket down the hall. Mom said it was immaturity and he'd grow out of it. But he never hurt anyone. He wouldn't do that.

He wrenched open the door and flung himself outside. He stomped around the car, then kicked it twice.

I took a long, deep breath, trying to steady my racing heart. Panic would do us no good. We had to think clearly. Logically. And no matter how difficult it was, because we drove each other crazy, we had to work *together*.

Someone started honking. "Hey, move your car."

Tyler put the car into neutral and we pushed it into a parking space.

I was about to sink back onto the seat when I

remembered something. "She has my phone," I said with a gasp. "Yes, that's it. She has my phone!" I'd given Jax my phone before we'd entered the museum. She'd used it to text us, to tell us when the security system had been disabled. I held out my hand. "Give me your phone. I'll call her."

"Are you nuts? You can't call her," Tyler said, his face flushed. "That phone is her best chance. If it rings, Ricardo will take it away. Hopefully she's turned it off and hidden it so she can use it later." He pulled his phone from his pocket. "But maybe we can trace her."

"That won't work," I said, my chest deflating. I took off my baseball cap and wiped my forehead with my sleeve. "I turned off the GPS, remember? So Ricardo couldn't track us. But maybe she'll turn it back on."

"Maybe." He shrugged. "Who are we kidding? Ricardo kidnapped her. He's not stupid. He'll search for a phone. She won't be able to call and we won't be able to track her."

The sounds of the city moved around us. People talking, cars honking, bus brakes screeching. Though Boston was populated by hundreds of thousands of people, I'd never felt so alone. "We have no choice. We have to tell the police," I said. "She's in danger."

"We've already been over this. No police. The urns are too dangerous. We can't let the government get hold of them." Tyler leaned against the car. Then he ran a hand through his hair. "I think Jax will be okay. She's not alone. Pyrrha will take care of her."

I wanted to believe that.

We'd met Pyrrha just a few days ago. We didn't know anything about her, except that she was a character from a famous myth, and she lived in the Realm of the Gods. She'd traveled through a magical portal to come to our world. It's difficult for me to admit, but all of that is true.

"What makes you think we can trust Pyrrha?" I asked. "She lied to us. She didn't tell us that Ricardo was her father."

"I trust her."

"That's just because you have a crush on her."

He frowned. Then his phone buzzed. I pressed close to him so I could read the screen. The message was from Ricardo.

Bring me the urn of Hope and the urn of Love and you shall have Jax. Otherwise, you will never see her again.

I tried to control the panic that welled in my chest. "Never see her?"

Tyler's phone buzzed again.

Both urns or no deal.

Tyler stared at the screen.

I tried taking a deep breath, but it didn't make me feel less anxious. My nose began to tingle, the sure sign of an imminent nosebleed. "Zeus has the urn of Hope. How are we supposed to get it?" Another text came in.

Bring the urns to the Eastern State Penitentiary by 8 a.m. tomorrow morning.

"What?" I screeched. "Get both urns by eight in the morning? No way. That's impossible."

"I'm texting him back." Tyler's thumbs flew over the keypad.

"Tell him that Zeus has Hope. That it's been destroyed! Tell him we can't get it."

"Such a move would be strategically ill-advised," Tyler grumbled. "He wants both urns and the fact that he wants something is what's going to keep Jax alive." Then he typed, **We need more time.**

Tyler pressed *send* but a *not delivered* message appeared. He tried to send it again. "Brilliant," Tyler grumbled. "He's limited our communication so we can't negotiate or change the parameters of his demands."

"The Eastern State Penitentiary is all the way in Philadelphia," I said. "That's like five hours away."

"I wonder why he wants to meet us at a prison?" Tyler asked.

"It used to be a prison," I told him. "Now it's a museum." But whether a prison, museum, or hot dog cart, the location didn't matter if we couldn't get the urn of Hope. "Jax," I whispered. The cousin I'd grown up with. My best friend. I might never see her again.

"And why eight a.m.?" Tyler wondered. "No villain ever sets up a meeting for eight a.m. It's always midnight. Or three a.m. when it's still dark. Are we going to make the exchange over coffee and doughnuts? What's the matter with him? Doesn't he ever read comic books?"

"I'll be sure to ask him that just before he opens the urn of Faith and *destroys the world*," I said sarcastically.

Despite how stressed out I felt, my nose hadn't started bleeding. But a drop of sweat rolled down it. The late afternoon sun was beating on us without mercy. My right hand was sticky with sweat. I opened it. I'd been holding the urn of Love this entire time, afraid to let it go. It was small. About the size of a plum. And bright red. "If we tell Ricardo the truth, that the urn of Hope is gone, he has no choice but to settle for this one," I suggested. "We'll give it to him. Then he won't hurt Jax."

Tyler looked at me and I could tell he was as scared as I was. This was no ordinary man we were dealing with. He'd robbed some banks. A person had been killed in the process. And now we knew that he'd come from the Realm of the Gods. He was an immortal and he had an ominous goal—to conquer the world.

Our world.

"We can't give him the urn of Love," Tyler said. "We can't allow him to hurt anyone else. It has to be destroyed. Do you hear me? *Destroyed.*" He grabbed my shoulder, his grip tight. His eyes were full of determination. There'd be no changing Tyler's mind. He knew the power of the urns. He'd been attacked by Hope and he'd barely survived. "We have to destroy *all* the urns *and* save Jax."

That sounded impossible.

Tyler reached into the backseat and grabbed a satchel. It was a leather bag with a golden trident stamped on the side. "Pyrrha left us the key to the portal. She wants us to return the urn, remember?"

"But—"

"I'll travel through the portal and give the urn of Love to Zeus, so he can destroy it, just as he destroyed Hope. Then I'll ask for Zeus's help. He'll want to punish Ricardo for stealing the urns. I'll make a deal with Zeus—if he helps us get Jax back, I'll tell him where to find Ricardo."

Make a deal with Zeus? This was unbelievably crazy. But what other choice did we have?

Trying to save my cousin *and* the world was not a usual day for me. I'm no superhero. I'm just a kid who goes to Chatham Middle School, and my brother is a gaming nerd who wins math competitions. We were supposed to be driving home. Our parents were expecting us. Jax's mom was waiting for her. To make matters worse, I had an allergy appointment on Wednesday. But instead, we were going to travel through a magical portal, into another dimension.

Tyler found the insurance card in the glove box. Then he called roadside service.

"Don't worry," he told me. "Jax isn't alone. Pyrrha will protect her."

He seemed convinced of Pyrrha's loyalty. But I wasn't so sure.

3
JAX

"Father, you seem different," Pyrrha said.

She looked just like a character from a myth, in her blue tunic and brown leather sandals that wound up to her knees. Her red hair sparkled even when the sun wasn't shining. I was so mad I scooted away. We were supposed to be working together. But she'd gone to the other side. The dark side. She'd joined Ricardo's team.

He sat across from us, his back to the driver. He didn't say hello. He didn't hug Pyrrha or tell her that he'd missed her. But I could tell that something had changed. When he saw her, his shoulders relaxed. His fingers stopped twitching. Even his voice softened. "You are here to join me?" he asked.

Pyrrha didn't pause to think about her answer. "Yes," she said.

"Are you kidding?" I asked, jerking around to face her. I'd been hoping that this was all a big fat misunderstanding. That she'd yell at him and tell him he was a terrible father and that he should stop trying to take over the world. That's what I'd tell my dad if he was trying to take over the world. "You're really going to *join* him?"

She ignored me. She looked deep into Ricardo's eyes. "Father, stop this chariot and let Jacqueline Malone go. Please. You do not need her. She is a mere mortal."

My stomach clenched. Was that an insult? "Hey," I said. "I'm not *mere*. There's nothing *mere* about me." Then I wondered if I actually knew what that word meant. And then I realized that maybe I'd said the wrong thing. "Uh, I think Pyrrha's right. If I'm a mere mortal, then I'm no use to you at all. So go ahead and stop the car and I'll jump out."

Ricardo's eyes narrowed. Clearly, he did not like this request. Whatever emotions he'd felt at being reunited with his daughter disappeared. His body stiffened again. The steely gaze returned. Evil Ricardo was back. "Do not underestimate the usefulness of mere mortals," he told Pyrrha. "They are proving to be quite pliable creatures. Easy to mold. Like clay in my hands." He rubbed his hands together. I expected one of those "muh ha ha" laughs.

He was really creeping me out. His slick black hair and pointed goatee made him look like a comic-book villain. Or one of those guys who would tie a woman to the train tracks in an old cowboy movie. Pyrrha looked nothing like him. Her total lack of creepiness must have come from her mom's side of the family. "You're not molding me!" I said defiantly. I reached across Pyrrha's lap and jabbed the unlock button. Panic was starting to stab at my chest. Maybe the lives of mere mortals meant nothing to them. We were just little ants to be stepped on. Pyrrha had pretended to be our friend, but she really didn't care about us. She wanted to rule the world too!

I jabbed again and again. "Let me out!"

"Father, please release—"

"Silence!" he bellowed. His eyes flashed as if little lightbulbs had exploded behind his irises.

Pyrrha stopped pleading. I shrank back against my seat. Panic turned to fear and for a moment I thought I might throw up.

When he spoke again, his voice was steady, but as intimidating as ever. "Pyrrha, you are free to go if you so choose. I will not stop you from returning to your mother. However, if you stay, I will welcome you as my daughter, and you shall become part of my glorious plan. But I will expect your loyalty to me, and not to *the gods*." He cringed as he said those last two words. "Do you understand?"

She nodded.

"Jacqueline, on the other hand, is not free to go until my conditions are met." He moved his fedora aside and calmly folded his hands on his lap. His frosty gaze settled on me. "I have full confidence that Tyler and Ethan Hoche will be successful. Two urns for the life of their cousin seems a fair price, to be delivered to me by eight a.m. tomorrow morning. But if they are unsuccessful, well, the life of one mortal girl means nothing in the grand scheme of things."

I decided that if I did throw up, I'd aim it right at him!

We were moving quickly now, zipping past other cars. I didn't know the area so I had no idea where we were.

"I know that you and your cousins possess the urn of Hope. And I highly suspect that you might possess the urn of Love, or at least know where it is. Therefore I am confident that they will deliver both urns to me." He paused. "What were you doing in the museum?" He was still staring at me. Didn't he ever blink?

"Looking around," I said, trying to sound bored. I hadn't actually looked at anything in the Museum of Fine Arts. I'd spent the whole time in the women's bathroom, disabling the security system. But I'd been in enough museums to take a good guess. "You know, paintings, statues, stuff like that." I shrugged. "My cousin Ethan wanted to go there. He's a total nerd. He loves history. To tell you the truth, I was really bored." Did he believe me? I couldn't tell. He seemed to wear one expression—menacing.

It was starting to get warm in there. I wanted to take off my purple jacket but I was afraid I might expose the hidden phone.

"Why did you leave the museum before your cousins?"

"I was bored," I repeated. "I told them I'd meet them outside. Jeez, what is this? An interrogation? Can't a person visit a stupid museum?"

It seemed like a good lie, but I knew it wouldn't work. Pyrrha had joined his side. She'd tell him the truth—that we'd gone into the Museum of Fine Arts to find the urn of Love so we could return it to Zeus and have it destroyed. I held my breath, waiting for her to say something.

"It is true, Father," she said innocently. "We were going to meet Jax outside. Ethan wanted to see the museum. He said there were many Greek artifacts that might interest me. I was not impressed. I preferred the Egyptian wing."

I took a slow breath. What was she doing? Why was she lying to him? She'd said nothing about the urn of Love. Had they found it? Or was it still inside the museum? I had no way of knowing. But she hadn't told him anything about it. Was she still on our side after all?

"Father," she said. "I came here to find you. I will not return to our realm without you. We can beg Zeus for forgiveness. And then we can be a family again." Her voice began to waver, as if she might cry. "Mother and I have missed you."

His jaw clenched. A little vein throbbed at the corner. Then, he erupted. "I will beg *no one* for forgiveness!" The limousine filled with his rage. His words echoed off the ceiling and floor. One of the windows cracked. I'd heard of opera singers hitting high notes and breaking wine glasses, but I'd never heard of anyone breaking a car window with words!

I shrank against my seat. But Pyrrha didn't flinch. Maybe she was used to his temper.

A few moments later, the echoes died away. Ricardo took a deep breath, his voice once again controlled and emotionless. "Tyler and Ethan Hoche will do whatever has to be done to save Jacqueline's life. They will deliver the urns to me." He gazed out the window, a faraway look on his face. Was he imagining his future world? What did it look like? Once he took over, would he crown himself a king? An emperor? "I have spent far too much time chasing after the urns," he said. "By assigning the labor to Tyler and Ethan, I will be free to prepare."

"Prepare?" Pyrrha asked.

"Not now," he said curtly. "We will discuss things in private. There is no need to involve this . . . *mortal girl.*"

I felt insulted again. "Hello? I'm already *involved.* You kidnapped me, remember?"

He ignored me. And Pyrrha didn't look at me either. Maybe it was best for me to be quiet. Mom was always telling me that sometimes you learn more by listening. "Father, what if Tyler and Ethan fail?" Pyrrha asked. "What if they can't find the urn of Love?"

"I will not waiver. Two urns or she dies."

Silence filled the limousine. I looked out the window. We were on a freeway now, leaving Boston behind.

I pulled my feet onto the seat and wrapped my arms around my knees. Two urns equaled my freedom. But one urn had already been destroyed. My freedom would not be given.

It looked like there was only one thing to do—I would have to free myself.

4
ETHAN

FACT: *Urns are some of the oldest relics that archaeologists have discovered. They were often used to hold cremated remains. In ancient Greece they were used to hold oil, and in early Anglo-Saxon tribes, a dead king's heart was sometimes placed in an urn.*

In modern mathematics, an urn problem is a thought experiment in probability theory. What that means is the experimenter comes up with a possible action, then explores the potential consequences of that action. It's a mental exercise, so the action doesn't have to be taken. You just have to think it through. I like thinking things through.

We couldn't save Jax, not yet. Tyler needed to go to the Realm of the Gods and ask Zeus for help.

Well, actually, Tyler wanted to make a trade with Zeus—if Zeus agreed to help us free Jax, Tyler would tell him where to find Ricardo. Tyler wanted to barter with a god.

How many consequences could that action have?

Roadside assistance showed up an hour later with a container of gas. Even though our portal to the gods wasn't far, I argued that we should stop at the first station to fill the rest of the tank. The way things were going, we never knew when we were going to end up in a car chase. During this whole trip I'd been in the backseat, acting as the map reader. That's what I'm comfortable with, looking up things on my phone. The fact-checker. The reader. But now I sat in the front seat, cradling the small red urn.

A long time ago, Zeus had filled the urn with love. It was a gift, given to Pyrrha. If she was feeling sad, she could open the urn and surround herself with love. He'd also given her urns filled with hope and faith. But the urns had been ruined by Pyrrha's father—the man we'd come to know as Ricardo. He'd opened the urns and had tainted them with wickedness and jealousy. So love escaped. As did hope and faith. The urns had been lying empty and abandoned for centuries. And as time passed, they began to crave love, hope, and faith the way a thirsty person craves water. They wanted to be filled again. If opened, they would steal love, faith, and hope from anyone standing nearby, ripping those feelings right out of a person's soul.

If I opened the urn of Love, everyone at the gas station would become its victim. What would it be like to be emptied of love? To see Mom and Dad and feel nothing. To watch Jax drive away and feel nothing. To watch Tyler collapse when the urn of Hope was unleashed on him and feel *nothing*.

It was a horrid thought.

Tyler was losing his temper again. "Why doesn't this fill faster?" He tried to shove the nozzle deeper into the tank. Gas fumes drifted in through the window.

I wasn't going to tell him to calm down. The

situation was crazy. He was filling the tank so we could drive to a portal that would take him to the Realm of the Gods. Which was located in another dimension. I was so nervous, I felt like I might cry and laugh at the same time.

I gripped the warm urn.

"We have to save Jax," I told him when he finally got back into the car.

"I know we have to save Jax! Tell me something I don't know." I could have told him lots of things he didn't know. My brain was a fact machine. But now was not the time. He started the engine, then drove back onto the road.

We didn't have far to go. It only took ten minutes to reach Boston Common, but it took ten more minutes for Tyler to find a parking space. It was crowded and despite his ability to calculate the position of figures and the properties of space, he was the worst at parallel parking.

"What are we going to tell Mom and Dad?" I asked.

"We tell them *nothing*," Tyler said. The scent of gasoline stung my eyes. In his hurry, he'd spilled some on his hands. "We lie."

"Lie?" I didn't think my stomach could clench any tighter. But it did and I wondered if I was too young for an ulcer. "We can't keep lying."

"Au contraire, little bro. We have to keep lying." He frowned at me. "Seriously, what would be worse? To get caught in a lie, or to never see Jax again?" It was a rhetorical question, of course. He grabbed his phone off the dashboard. "I'll text Dad and say we're having car trouble and we need to stay one more day." He shrugged. "It's partially true. We did have to call roadside service."

"You think we can do this by eight a.m.?" I asked.

"Jeez, how am I supposed to know? I've never traveled to another dimension before. Well, I have, in my game." Tyler and two of his friends had been creating a game called Cyclopsville that takes place in the Realm of the Gods. As far as coincidences go, this one was pretty weird.

"They expect us home tonight," I reminded him. It was Sunday. Mom was away on a business trip, but Dad had let us drive to Boston to attend a comic-book festival. He's a big comic-book fan. Our parents knew nothing about the urns, or Ricardo. "I'll pretend my battery is dying," Tyler said as he began to text. "I'll tell Dad not to worry and that we'll call tomorrow when the car is fixed and my phone is recharged. I'll tell him we're going to spend more time at the festival."

It all sounded good. Dad wasn't a worrier. He'd want us to have fun at the festival. Mom worried mostly about the amount of time Tyler spent on the computer in the virtual world with his friends, and the amount of time I spent in the real world *not* making friends. But in this case, Tyler wasn't on his computer and I was being social. Maybe Mom would see the extra day as a positive.

If there was one person who could be given the title "worrier," it was me. I was making a mental list of all the things that could go wrong. We had no idea what traveling to another dimension might do to Tyler's body. Was gravity the same? Did they have the same oxygen-to-carbon ratio we had here? Were there odd diseases that Tyler hadn't been immunized against?

"Done," Tyler announced. Then he shoved his phone into his pocket. It was dinnertime and Tyler hadn't mentioned food, which was unusual. His stomach was like a black hole. "Aren't you hungry?"

"No."

"Don't you want a burger or something?"

"Nope."

I was stalling. "Shouldn't we talk about this more?" I pleaded. Both my palms were sweating so

I set the urn on my lap. "Shouldn't we try texting Ricardo again, just in case?"

Okay, Tyler typed, **Do not hurt Jax. We're going to get your urns.** But, just like last time, the text went undelivered. "Ricardo doesn't want to give us any power," he said. "We have to wait for him to contact us." Tyler looked at the urn and his expression turned stormy. "We *will* save Jax."

"How?"

"I don't know. You can't always have a plan, Ethan. Sometimes you just have to go for it." He opened the door.

I didn't like not having a plan.

5

TYLER

Welcome to the Game.

You are logged in as Tyler. You are seventeen years old, in excellent health aside from a few hunger pangs. Aside from the urn of Love, which you should not open under any circumstances, you are unarmed and there are no weapons currently available. Your strength resides in your superior intellect.

Your objectives: Deliver the urn of Love to Zeus so that it can be destroyed. Convince Zeus to help free your cousin, Jax, from the clutches of the archvillain Ricardo, aka Epimetheus.

And finally, save Pyrrha, the girl of your dreams.

This is a solo mission.

Your location is a portal through which you will enter the Realm of the Gods.

You have until eight a.m. tomorrow morning to complete your mission.

Start Game.

6
ETHAN

FACT: *We exist in three-dimensional space. We can move up and down, sideways, we can step in and out. The space we move in can be measured. But the English philosopher, John G. Bennett, thought that there were three more dimensions that we couldn't see and one of these was called eternity. Eternity was a timeless time, immeasurable, and that's where Tyler was going.*

Boston Common was a large public park in the middle of Boston. Even though it was dinnertime, the park was filled with people. A group of Peruvians were performing on their flutes and selling CDs. A professional dog walker nearly ran us over as her pack of mutts spotted a squirrel. A family walked past. The little boy was carrying a plastic sword and attacking the bushes. I thought of Tyler's sword collection. Tyler, who was walking quickly, didn't seem to notice the kid. I guess I was looking for distractions—anything to keep my mind from focusing on the facts.

I followed Tyler down a path to a fountain. It was called Brewer Fountain. Four large bronze statues sat at the base, water spouting past their shoulders. Tyler had told us their stories. The young man and woman had been in love, but a jealous Cyclops had killed the man, smashing him with a boulder. So much blood ran from his dead body that it formed a river, which was named after him. The Acis River. The older pair was the god of the sea, Poseidon, and his sea-nymph wife. Yesterday we'd watched Pyrrha stand in front of Poseidon and disappear into thin air. She'd reappeared a few hours later, her hair in a different style and dressed in new clothes. I know this is a cliché but I wouldn't have believed it if I hadn't seen it with my own two eyes.

The Poseidon statue was a portal of some sort, leading to the Realm of the Gods. Pyrrha told us that she'd traveled through the portal and that she'd given the urn of Hope to Zeus and that it had been destroyed. It was great news, especially for Tyler, who'd been a victim of the urn. Then Pyrrha surprised Tyler with a gift—a small vial of green liquid. Even though Tyler had insisted that he'd recovered from the effects of having hope drained from his soul, Pyrrha had sensed that some sadness still lingered. Tyler drank the elixir and he was back to his old, snarky self. That's when I really knew that it wasn't a magic trick. Pyrrha was the real deal.

Just when we reached the fountain, Tyler's phone buzzed. "Is it Ricardo?" I asked, my heart skipping a beat.

"It's Dad," he said, reading the screen. "He says, 'Glad you're having fun. I'm working on a project at the office. Call tomorrow when you're on your way home.'"

It was a huge relief to know that Dad wasn't worried. We were in the clear for one more night. But I wished that we'd hear from Jax.

Tyler texted back, **Thanks**. Then he stared at the fountain. "Okay, so I'll go into the portal and tell Zeus what's going on."

"And then what?"

"I still don't know," he said. "Hopefully he'll help us. Maybe he'll come back with me and deal with Ricardo face-to-face. But in any case, I'll meet you here as soon as I can."

He didn't seem one bit nervous. He was acting like this was an ordinary outing—like he was going into a Starbucks to get a latte. But he was about to step into a world populated by mythological creatures! "What if it's not that easy?" I asked. "Zeus is the king of the gods. What if he's too busy to help? Or doesn't care about finding Ricardo anymore?"

Tyler scratched his chin. "Well, if he doesn't care about Ricardo, he might still care about Pyrrha. I'll tell him that she's in danger. I'll tell him that she's been kidnapped."

"You're going to lie to Zeus?" My stomach was clenching again. Technically, Pyrrha hadn't been taken hostage. She'd volunteered to jump into Ricardo's car.

"Do you want to save Jax or not?" he snapped.

I didn't need to answer that question.

He handed me the car keys. "Just in case," he said.

"Just in case what?"

"In case I don't make it back."

I gulped. Then I took the keys. He didn't bother rolling up his jeans, or taking off his shoes. And he didn't look around to see if anyone was watching. He stepped into the fountain.

"Hey," I said. "Now that I think about it, shouldn't we both go?" I didn't want to go, but I didn't want to be left alone, either. "I mean, what if you need my help . . . over there?"

Over there. In another dimension. This was crazy. Should I bring a suitcase? Should I bring an extra inhaler, in case I'm allergic to Pegasus dander? Who knows what kind of pollen floats around in eternity?

"You'd better take this, too." He handed me his phone. "I doubt the gods have cell towers." I laughed, but I was so nervous, it came out as a strangled squeak. I clutched the phone and keys in one hand. My other hand was still cupping the urn of Love. "If I don't come back, you'll be the only person who will know what happened to Jax," Tyler said. "And what happened to me."

We looked at each other. Tyler and I had never been super close. He wasn't the kind of older brother who'd held my hand when I was a toddler. Or who'd included me in any of his activities. He'd ignored me, much of the time. Though we lived in the same house, we'd lived very separate lives. But the events of the summer had brought us closer. Because of the urn of Hope, Tyler had almost died and that had been the worst thing I'd ever experienced. But now here we were, talking about the possibility of never seeing each other again.

Having me stay behind made perfect, logical sense. I was the only link between Jax, Ricardo, Tyler, and Great-Aunt Juniper. If both Tyler and I disappeared, Mom and Dad might never know what became of us.

"Hey, kid, there's no swimming in the fountain," an old man called.

We ignored him. "How long should I wait for you?" I asked.

"I don't know. As long as you can. You might have to lie to Mom and Dad some more."

"Be careful," I told him. No one had to remind *me* about not taking unnecessary risks. But Tyler and I were as different as night and day. He stepped in puddles without considering their depth. He walked right into the middle of a crowd without making sure there were nearby exits. He even used public ketchup bottles. Risk aversion was definitely not part of his DNA sequencing.

I handed him the urn of Love. Without another word, he turned away and started walking across the fountain, toward Poseidon. I wanted to offer him some advice. But what could I say?

"Try not to make Zeus mad!" I hollered. Tyler was good at many things, but he was an expert on annoying people. Most of the gamers I'd met were annoying. They had opinions, and if you didn't know what obscure fantasy character they were referring to, or a particular episode of *Doctor Who*, they acted like you were stupid. If Tyler and Zeus got into a conversation and Zeus didn't know anything about online, multiplayer formats, Tyler might insult him. "And don't lose the bag or you can't get back!"

Tyler whipped around. "The bag!" he cried. "I left it in the car!"

Oh. My. God! "I'll get it!"

I ran as fast as I could. It took me exactly 3.3 minutes to get to our parking spot. I unlocked the car and grabbed Pyrrha's leather bag. I relocked the car and ran, the bag slung over my shoulder. By the time I made it back, I was completely out of breath. Luckily, no one seemed to care that Tyler was still standing in the fountain. "Hey!" I called, holding up the bag.

Unfortunately, the Peruvian band was now standing on the pathway, quite close to Tyler. The drums were loud enough to drown out my voice. Tyler stared at Poseidon like he was in some kind of trance.

Trying not to think about the fact that some of the worst diseases that inflict mankind are carried by filthy water, I climbed into the basin, and sloshed up to him. "Here!"

He pointed at the statue. "Look."

Like the other three statues, Poseidon sat on a ledge. He wore a laurel wreath on his head. His beard was long and wavy, and his chest was bare. He sat with his hand resting on his knee, his face turned toward his sea-nymph wife, who sat on another ledge. What was I supposed to be looking at? Nothing seemed unusual.

"There!" Tyler said, his finger jabbing the air in front of Poseidon's eyes.

A slight flicker of light came from inside the bronze eyes. I shivered.

Then I looked at the bag. The golden trident had begun to glow. The bag was vibrating. I shoved the car keys and the phone into my pocket. Then I yanked the bag off my shoulder. "It's starting to do something!" I hollered as the flute-playing reached an obnoxious volume. "Take it! Hurry!"

Tyler grabbed the bag but before I let go, the ground disappeared and I fell into darkness.

7

JAX

We drove in silence for a long while. Ricardo was busy texting. He sure had a lot to say because his thumbs were flying. With his gaze focused on his screen, I took the opportunity to sneak a closer look at him. He didn't have any wrinkles on his face, and no crow's-feet around his eyes, so even though I knew he was Pyrrha's dad, he seemed young. My mom has a special cream she puts on at night, to fill the lines around her eyes. I guess being immortal meant you didn't need to worry about things like that. As I thought about my mom, an ache spread across my chest. Would I ever see her again? Tears waited, pushing at the corners of my eyes. I clenched my fists, refusing to cry. I would get out of this situation. I *would* see Mom again.

"It's stuffy in here," I complained. "Can we roll down the window?"

Without looking up, Ricardo tapped on the driver's glass screen. A moment later, my window rolled down two inches and a breeze trickled in. I felt like a dog, pointing my nose at the crack, and inhaling the cool air. I hadn't realized how much I'd been sweating.

Pyrrha was sitting quietly, also watching her father. "Mother misses you," she said. He didn't respond. "She wants you to come home. She is going to speak to Zeus and—"

"Zeus?" He looked up. His eyes were freaky. They seemed to change color with his moods. At that moment, a gray storm churned around his pupils. "Zeus is irrelevant. He banished himself from this land. The people no longer worship him. In this world, Zeus is found only in museums."

"And in books," I said. I'd checked one out at the Chatham Public Library. Not my usual reading material but hey, when you're thrust into a Greek god soap opera, you might as well do some research.

He dismissed my comment with a wave of his hand. "Once I have claimed this world, Zeus's name will be erased from history. All images of him will be destroyed. All literary references will also be destroyed." He sounded totally confident. As if Zeus were a bug on the sidewalk and all he had to do was step on him.

"Uh, just so you know, burning books doesn't work around here. People keep trying it, but the stories always survive."

He finally blinked. Had I struck some kind of nerve?

Then his voice turned so cold, I swear the air turned cold too. "I shall be victorious, and the memory of Zeus will dissolve like dust in water."

Wow, he really hated Zeus.

Greek mythology had never meant that much to me. Tyler was the expert on the subject. Most of the games he played had something to do with the mythological world. Even that card game tournament he'd won, Magic: The Gathering, was full of Greek gods and monsters. Tyler and his friends played the game at Merlin's comic-book store.

They'd be devastated if Ricardo burned the place down. "No matter how much you don't like Zeus, you can't erase history," I said.

Was that a smile at the corner of his mouth? "Of course I can," he told me, as if speaking to the stupidest person on Earth. "Civilizations are erased by conquerors and new civilizations arise time and time again."

I was beginning to realize that Ricardo was actually crazy.

Pyrrha had been quietly observing her dad. Was she also realizing that he was crazy? Or maybe she already knew. "What about Mother?" she asked sadly. "Do you not miss her? Do you not want to see her again?"

"Pandora is free to come here and join me."

"You know she cannot do that. It is against Zeus's laws."

"In this new world, only my laws will matter." Then he looked at his phone and began texting again. It was weird to see a villain do something as commonplace as send a text. But I suppose his texts were anything but commonplace. They probably included the words *destroy*, *terrorize*, and *doom*. Pyrrha sighed with frustration. There would be no reasoning with him.

As much as Ricardo hated Zeus, I was beginning to hate Ricardo. Not just because he was hurting people; he'd kidnapped me, and he was planning on taking over the world. But also because he'd hurt my own family in a very personal way. While I was seriously afraid of him, and knew I should probably shut up, I wanted to know the truth. "Why is my dad in jail?" I asked.

He stopped texting. An eyebrow raised, but no answer came. Was he going to pretend he didn't know what I was talking about?

"My father, Isaac Romero, is in the Brookville Federal Prison Camp. He was working for the International Society of Archaeologists, with my great-aunt, and then he was arrested for theft. But he didn't do it."

Up until last month I hadn't known my father's name. Mom thought he'd abandoned us when I was a baby. Before she had her stroke, Great-Aunt Juniper told me all about him. He was called the Locksmith because he was an expert on creating elaborate security systems. But he'd been unfairly arrested and had spent most of my life in prison. Because I was curious about him, and because he'd worked with Great-Aunt Juniper, we'd driven to Brookville to meet him and to get information about the urns.

"He's in prison because of you. You set him up," I said. Part of me was really scared at that moment. I'd just accused a madman of sending an innocent man to jail. But the other part of me wanted justice for my dad, so I looked Ricardo right in his immortal eyes. "Why?"

His mouth tightened and that vein appeared again. He knew exactly what I was talking about. "The Locksmith is a brilliant man," he said.

He was complimenting my dad? I hadn't been expecting that reaction. "Are you telling me you set him up because he's smarter than you?" His eyes flashed again and I cringed. Maybe I shouldn't have said that.

He sat back against his seat, crossed his right leg over his left, and gave me his full-on attention. I suddenly felt very small. "You are a talkative creature," he said.

"So I've been told." I stuck my hands into the pockets of my purple jacket, so he wouldn't see that they'd started trembling. "But I want answers."

Pyrrha was listening, but remained silent.

A strand of black hair fell across Ricardo's forehead. He pushed it aside. "The Locksmith was assisting Juniper, making it difficult for me to retrieve my urns. I needed to *relocate* him, so he could no longer interfere with my quest." A pang of sadness hit me. Tyler loved that word—*quest*. Would I ever see my cousins again? Ricardo sneered. "I needed to eliminate him."

Relocate? Eliminate? "So it's true. My dad didn't steal anything."

One corner of Ricardo's mouth turned up. Just a little. Just enough for me to know that he was proud of himself. He pressed his fingertips together. "How very easy it is to control the minds of mortals. When the Mask of Agamemnon disappeared from the National Archaeological Museum in Athens, it took little effort to convince the Athenian police chief to put a few fingerprints exactly where they needed to be *placed*."

Of course! Ricardo had used the urn of Faith on the police chief. He'd sent my father to prison.

My face felt real hot and my vision got blurry as tears stung my eyes. Ricardo had ruined my dad's life! My mom's life! My life!

Pyrrha reached out to touch my shoulder but

54

I pulled away. I stared out the window. We were still on the freeway. It was starting to get dark. I'd missed dinner and my stomach felt hollow. How long had we been driving? I wasn't wearing a watch and couldn't check the time on Ethan's phone.

I rested my head against the glass. At the first chance, I'd make a run for it. As soon as that door opened I'd bolt out of that limo at lightning speed. But if I had to defend myself, I would. When I was in third grade I went to martial arts camp. We learned a few things, like how to do a roundhouse kick. And we learned that there are three places on the body that are super vulnerable: the eyeballs, throat, and crotch. If I had to poke Ricardo in the eyes, I would. Even though that sounded gross. I'd do whatever it took.

But would Pyrrha try to stop me? Was she really on her dad's side? Was she willing to help him take over the world or was she just trying to save him? I had no idea. I didn't want to hurt her but if she got in my way . . .

If you push a wolf into a corner, you're gonna get bitten!

I curled up in the seat, trying to get comfortable. What were Tyler and Ethan doing? Were they trying to figure out how to rescue me? Even if they had both urns, they'd never give them to Ricardo. That wasn't even an option. Would they remember to talk to my mom so she wouldn't worry? She'd be home right now, waiting for me to call after a long day of work at the diner. I thought about the diner's pancakes. And the fluffy scrambled eggs and hot chocolate.

My eyelids felt heavy. My head snapped forward. Crud, I'd almost fallen asleep!

There was no way I would let myself fall asleep. I had to stay alert. Had to listen to everything Ricardo said. Had to watch where we were going so that when I texted Tyler and Ethan, I could tell them everything.

But it was so hard to keep my eyes open. Maybe I could close them, just for a moment.

Only a moment.

8
ETHAN

FACT: *When people die and are brought back to life, they often talk about seeing a light at the end of a tunnel. Some believe that the light is heaven. Some say it has to do with the brain's electrical impulses. When somebody is having a difficult time, they might get the advice, "Oh, don't worry, there's always a light at the end of the tunnel," meaning things will get better.*

I'm not so sure about that.

We stood in what looked like a long tunnel, but I couldn't be entirely certain because it was very dark in there. A pinprick of light glowed at the end, far away.

Here's what I knew. My shoes and socks were soaking wet. And I could barely see Tyler standing next to me, but I could hear him breathing.

"Where . . . ?" That was the only word I was able to utter. It felt as if I'd been punched in the stomach and I couldn't quite find my breath. That one word echoed down the stone walls.

Where? Where? Where?

"We're not in Kansas anymore," Tyler whispered. Then he let go of the bag and whipped around. "Hey, wait a minute. What are you doing here?" His booming voice echoed so loudly, I winced.

"I don't know," I said. "The bag was vibrating and I tried to hand it to you. And then . . ." I looked at my hand. "We were both holding on to it. Oh. My. God." My heart started to pound in my ears. I'd gone through the portal. The portal!

"You were supposed to stay in the park. This is supposed to be a solo mission. I can't believe you messed this up," Tyler grumbled.

"I didn't mess it up. You're the one who forgot the bag."

"Oh really? Just like I *forgot* to fill the gas tank,"

he said. I waited for the name-calling. Tyler preferred names that made it perfectly clear he believed he was my intellectual superior—moroon, brainsap, idjot were a few of his favorites. But this time he didn't insult me. Instead, he cleared his throat. "Okay, so maybe I did forget the bag, but you shouldn't have come with me. Jeez, Ethan, what's going to happen if we both get stuck here? Who's going to help Jax?"

"I don't know!" I yelled. "And stop yelling at me!"

Me. Me. Me.

I took a long breath. "I think we should stop fighting and figure out where we are." We both turned and faced the pinprick of light. I swallowed hard. "What do you remember?" I asked.

"The ground gave way," Tyler said. "It felt like I was falling."

"Me too."

"Vertigo is a classic symptom of interdimensional travel," Tyler said. "Or so I've read."

"Maybe we actually fell. Maybe we're below the fountain." I wanted desperately to still be in Boston.

"You mean like a trapdoor?"

"Yes, a trapdoor! Maybe we're under the park. This could be a drainage pipe, or an engineering tunnel, or something like that."

"There's only one way to find out." He handed me the urn of Love. "Carry this, will ya? It's making me sweat." Then he started walking toward the light.

"What are you doing?"

"I'm going to see what's at the end of this tunnel. But keep your voice low. If this is the Realm of the Gods, we don't know who might be out there. We'll have to sneak in."

Was it possible to sneak into the Realm of the Gods? "Don't you think the gods have special hearing powers? Besides, we *want* to find Zeus, remember?"

"Zeus, sure. But I don't want one of the monsters to find us first. Got it?"

Monsters? Plural?

As much as I didn't want to reach the end of the tunnel, I didn't want to be alone, either. I set the urn of Love into the leather bag and slung it over my shoulder. Then I followed my brother.

The tunnel went on forever. The light didn't seem to get any bigger. It was difficult to see and I kept tripping over stones. "You're walking too fast," I whispered. I thought about using the flashlight app on Tyler's phone, but I didn't want to attract any attention. Our wet sneakers made annoying squelching sounds but there was no way we could walk barefoot over the stones. My breathing began to sound wheezy. There was probably a lot of dust in the tunnel. Or mold spores. Or vermin dander. My skin prickled at the thought. Throughout history, rats have been the deliverers of plague. Whether I was still in Boston, in a tunnel below the fountain, or at the entryway to the Realm of the Gods, I didn't want to run into any rats. Or anything else that might like cold, damp places.

"Tyler? Do Cyclopses live in tunnels?"

"No. They're cave dwellers. Jeez, haven't you been paying attention to Cyclopsville?"

"What if this tunnel leads to a cave?" I imagined the Cyclops who ripped Acis apart and the torrent of blood that became the Acis River. It would be nice to have a river named after me but not under those circumstances.

"Shhh," he scolded.

I couldn't shake the feeling that something could sneak up on me at any moment, so I darted in front of Tyler. "No," he said, pushing me behind him. "It's safer back there."

He was right. I'd never been surprised by Tyler's ability to win math competitions or gaming tournaments, but his courage during this whole thing had shocked both me and Jax. He'd sacrificed himself to the urn of Hope to protect us. And now he was leading the way, into the unknown. He'd either wind up at the end of a drainage pipe in Boston Harbor, or he'd step into a realm that wasn't supposed to exist.

We had no plan. That's where it stood. We had goals—don't let Ricardo get the urns, and save Jax. But how were we going to pull them off? If we couldn't find Zeus, what would we do? Or worse, what if Zeus didn't want to help us? He probably had a very busy schedule overseeing the pantheon of gods. We didn't even have an appointment. If you want to see my allergist, you have to make an appointment at least six weeks in advance.

My legs started to get tired. I checked Tyler's phone to see how long we'd been walking but the clock wasn't working. And there was no way to make a call because there were zero bars. No surprise. Without a watch or the sky, it was really difficult to know how long we'd been inside the tunnel. It felt like hours had passed.

Finally, the light began to grow larger, and brighter. Tyler raised his hand to shield his eyes. Then the light seemed to envelop him and he disappeared. I reached out an arm. "Tyler?" I whispered. I took a few more steps, reaching, hoping to find Tyler's shoulder. But there was nothing. Had he fallen off a ledge? Or into the water? It was so bright I closed my eyes. "Tyler?"

A hand grabbed mine and pulled me forward. I stumbled over a few rocks, then stopped.

A warm breeze stroked my face and a lovely scent reminded me of summer. I opened my eyes.

9
JAX

S omeone nudged me awake.

"Huh?" I said, sitting up. It was dark, except for the glow of passing headlights. Pyrrha sat next to me on the leather bench seat, holding a water bottle. We were still in the back of the limo. Grogginess immediately washed away as I was flooded with cold, hard reality. "How long have I been asleep?"

"Hours," she said.

"Hours?" I rubbed crust out of my eyes. "Where's Ricardo?"

"He is sitting with the chariot driver."

Finally we were alone. We could talk! "What happened to—" I started to ask but she put a finger to her lips and her eyes darted toward the glass barrier that separated the driver's seat from ours. Ricardo could hear us. Of course.

I groaned. I wouldn't be able to ask her anything. However, with Ricardo up front, now was the time for me to contact Tyler and Ethan. I'd text them. Let them know I was okay. Find out what they were planning. But just as I reached for my phone, Pyrrha dropped her water bottle at my feet. She reached for it and as she did, she knocked my arm aside. "Oh, sorry," she said. As she grabbed the bottle, she whispered, "He can see us, too."

The phone would have to wait. I glared at the dark window. It was a one-way mirror. We were caged animals, being watched by a zookeeper. Maybe Ricardo was asleep up there, but maybe he wasn't. Did immortals need to sleep? Or eat? "I'm hungry," I murmured.

Pyrrha handed me a bottle of water from the minibar. "I am sorry but there is nothing more," she said.

I drank half the bottle. Staying hydrated would

help me stay alert. I couldn't fall asleep again and miss my chance to escape. I tried the door, just in case. But it was still locked. What was I going to do anyway—throw myself onto the freeway?

I still didn't know what Pyrrha was up to. She'd volunteered to get into this limo. She'd offered to help her dad. But at the same time, she hadn't told him that she knew where to find the urn of Love. She was keeping important information from him. If she was trying to trick both me *and* Ricardo, did that make her a double agent?

In a way, I understood Pyrrha's loyalty. We might have been totally different in appearance and in mortality. We even lived in different worlds. But we had one thing in common—our dads were criminals. Well, mine wasn't *technically* a criminal, but that's what it said on his permanent record. Pyrrha had come to this world because she wanted to save her dad from the mess he'd created. If I could, I'd save my dad too. But that was impossible. I couldn't unlock the prison and set him free.

The limo slowed down and we turned off the freeway. I unbuckled my seat belt and knelt on the seat so I could get a better look. The road was called Benjamin Franklin Parkway.

Philadelphia!

We took a right onto Twenty-Second Street and drove past the Philadelphia Museum of Art. There was no traffic on the street so it must have been super early in the morning. I wondered if the museum had a statue of Zeus. Or if Ricardo had already destroyed it. If he wanted to erase Zeus, he'd have to get rid of every piece of pottery, every painting, and all the books that contained references to Greek mythology. Then he'd have to go online and delete everything. Or change the definition of Zeus, so that when someone googled him, they'd get a brand-new meaning. But even if Ricardo did all that, he'd still have to wait generations for everyone to forget. Could he do that?

It seemed like an impossible goal. But since he was immortal, time was on his side.

We drove five blocks and turned onto Fairmount Avenue. One side of the street was lined with apartment buildings, all dark except for a few TVs glowing in windows. Probably people with insomnia. But the other side of the street was lined with a stone wall, too tall to climb over. It reminded me of the kind of wall that was built around a medieval fortress. I'd seen this wall in one of my guide books, highlighted as a place to visit, but I couldn't remember what it was.

Then the limo slowed. A sandwich board stood on the sidewalk in front of the wall. It read: *Eastern State Penitentiary Closed for Repairs*.

A penitentiary? I'd never visited a prison until I went to see my dad. Was I about to visit another?

I pressed against the window, trying to get a better view. The limo was idling in front of an entryway that was blocked by a metal gate. There was a red door next to the gate but it was closed. Two giant gargoyle statues perched above the gate, peering down at us. A tower rose behind them. This place looked more like a castle than a prison. Red lights flickered in the gargoyles' stone eyes. It was some kind of camera or motion detector.

The red door opened. Two men stepped out. They were dressed in blue suits and white shirts, and even though it was still dark outside, they both wore sunglasses. One of them walked up to the driver's door. The conversation was muffled. Then the gate opened and the limo pulled into the entry. We drove under an arch, past a ticket booth and a big sign that read: *Welcome to the Eastern State Penitentiary Museum*.

"What is this place?" Pyrrha asked.

"I can't remember," I told her. "Looks like it used to be a prison but now it's a museum." I suddenly missed Ethan. He was always full of historical facts. He had the kind of brain that remembered everything he'd ever read. I couldn't imagine having that kind of brain. It would be like a superpower. I wished I could google this place on his phone, but I didn't want to risk it.

We drove into an inner courtyard. The limo stopped; the engine shut off. Pyrrha and I looked at each other. I had no idea what would happen next. Would this be my chance to escape?

The back door opened. Pyrrha got out, then I followed. My hands were shaking. I stepped onto the concrete. My legs felt like jelly. The first thing I saw was a long building with metal bars over each of the windows. Was that where they'd kept the prisoners? Ricardo stood near the building, talking to another pair of guys who were also dressed in blue suits, white shirts, and dark glasses. Was that the uniform for the museum workers? It looked more like something an FBI or CIA agent might wear. My guidance counselor at school said I should consider working for a spy agency. I guess that was because I'd told her that I like to eaves-drop on strangers and try to uncover secrets about their lives. Hey, if someone is talking about a secret *in public*, I say it's fair game.

From the corner of my eye, I noticed that the gate had already closed. There'd be no escaping that way. But maybe I could slip through the red door.

"You have the report?" Ricardo asked. "The Paris Operation has been a success?"

"Yes sir," one of the men replied. Both were standing like soldiers at full attention.

"Excellent. And what about the preparations for the morning's grand ceremony?"

"Everything is in order."

"Very good. Follow me." Ricardo began to lead them toward a set of double doors.

Had he forgotten about us? What luck! I slowly began to back away. As soon as he entered that building, I'd run for the street.

But as if reading my mind, Ricardo turned swiftly on his heels and strode toward me. He held out his hand. "Your phone. I will take it now."

I gulped. Did he have some sort of godly X-ray vision? "I don't know what . . ." Then I realized there was no use lying. As I handed it over, I knew that I'd just given up my best chance at survival. And my only way to tell Mom I loved her, one last time. "Please," I said. "My mom will be worried. Please let me go."

His scowl relaxed. His eyes warmed. My plea had touched him. I could tell! Behind his cold mask, behind his evil shell, was there a person who felt pity?

"Please," I begged again.

"Yes, Father, please," Pyrrha said.

But the moment disappeared. "Jacqueline's mother should not have allowed her to travel all this way without supervision," he said. "Her fate is sealed."

I glared at him as hard as I could. "Why are we here? Why are we in this museum?"

"You are standing in my latest acquisition," he said, tucking Ethan's phone into his pocket.

Acquistion? Why would someone sell a museum to Ricardo? But then I guessed the answer. He probably didn't buy it. He probably took it. With the urn of Faith, he could convince anyone to do anything. What was next? The Grand Canyon? The White House? What was the Paris Operation he asked about? Was he buying the Eiffel Tower? He'd had the urn for many years. What other places had he *acquired*?

He adjusted his fedora. "I would give you a tour but I am not a tour guide," he told me, his upper lip curling into a sneer. "There are other matters to which I must attend. Pyrrha, you will join me."

"Yes, Father, I would like that," she said.

"As for you, Jacqueline, my driver, Timothy, will take you to a room where you will wait. If your cousins do as I have instructed, you will be free to go at eight a.m. If not, then I have . . ." He bent close and whispered, ". . . *other plans for you.*"

I tried not to flinch. Tried not to blink as he looked deep into my eyes. But I failed.

He motioned at the driver, who'd been standing silently in the shadows. Then the two men held open a pair of double doors, and Ricardo entered the long building.

Pyrrha gave me a worried look. *I'll find you*, she mouthed at me. Then she followed her father.

He has *other plans* for me? I don't think so.

As soon as Ricardo, Pyrrha, and the two men were out of sight, I ran toward the red door.

10
ETHAN

FACT: *According to the ancient Greek philosopher Aristotle, "time" is defined by change and movement. Where there is change taking place, there is time. Where there is movement, there is time. Everything that comes to be or ceases to be exists in time.*

But the gods are never changing and eternal, and thus exist outside time.

I was standing outside the tunnel, facing a field. Long stalks of purple lavender waved in the breeze, beneath a sky that was as blue as an Easter egg. Tyler stood next to me.

"Wow," he said.

"Wow," I echoed. There was no doubt in my mind. We were no longer in Boston.

"This place is amazing." Tyler laughed. "Give me my phone."

"But there's no signal," I told him.

"I'm gonna take pictures. Give it to me." He grabbed the phone from my pocket and started walking into the field, snapping photos of the sky, the grass, the trees. "Look at these colors!"

Everyone would think he'd photoshopped the pictures because the colors were much brighter here than back home—more saturated, more intense. The trees had pure white trunks, and emerald-green leaves. Patches of cherry-red flowers and lemon-yellow buttercups dotted the landscape. And everything seemed to glow. No clouds marred the perfect sky, yet the sun wasn't sweltering, and it wasn't muggy, like the summers in Chatham. I realized I didn't have sunblock, which worried me because I didn't tan as easily as Tyler. But the good news was that even though the grasses were full of seeds, I wasn't sneezing.

"Hey, these are fruit trees," Tyler called.

I looked around. Did I dare venture forth? There was no sign of other people. Or gods or monsters. Making sure the leather bag was secure, I headed toward Tyler. As I approached the first tree, I noticed an unusual sound. When the breeze rustled the tree's leaves, faint music was released. And when I took a deep breath, I inhaled air sweet with ripe fruit, like a pie baking in the oven. My worries began to fade away.

Tyler reached up and yanked a piece of fruit from a tree branch, then handed it to me. It was an apricot and its smooth skin was warm from the sun. Then he picked one for himself. "Wait," I warned, but he'd already taken a bite.

"OMG. This is the best thing I've ever tasted." A piece of apricot skin clung to his teeth as he smiled.

Something felt weird to me. Why did Tyler look so happy? We were in the middle of a huge crisis. I stepped closer to him and looked into his eyes. I thought about Odysseus, from the famous book *The Odyssey*. His goal was to get home to his family, but during his journey, some of his crew ate fruit that made them forget about going home. They were held captive by an evil enchantment. I dropped my apricot on the ground. "Tyler?"

"Huh?" He took another bite.

"You look different all of a sudden. You look . . . happy."

"Of course I'm happy. I'm in the Realm of the Gods, dude. *We're* in the Realm of the freakin' Gods!"

"I know but you're smiling like you're drunk or something." I pointed to the apricot pit in his hand. "Do you think . . . ?"

"Do I think what?" He looked at the pit. "Oh, you mean like Odysseus?" He dropped it, then plucked another apricot. "I'm not under a spell. I haven't forgotten why we're here. I remember everything. Ricardo. Jax. The urns. Don't worry. I'm just savoring the moment."

I sighed with relief. I was hungry too, so I picked an apricot. Tyler hadn't been exaggerating. It was like eating warm pie! The juice dribbled down my chin. "You know what?" I asked, looking at my shoes. "My pants and shoes aren't wet anymore." They'd been drenched from the fountain but only a few minutes in this place and they were dry.

Tyler began to climb the tree. "What are you doing?" I asked.

"I'm going to get a better view," he said. "Jeez,

Ethan, think of all the research I could do! This is a once-in-a-lifetime opportunity to make Cyclopsville as realistic as possible. I need to take mental notes on the landscape, the architecture, anything that can be used in our game. And if I could see a real Cyclops, that would be killer!"

"Uh, that sounds dangerous," I mumbled. Even from a safe distance, a real Cyclops could hurl a boulder at us. Or something equally deadly. "Don't they toss sheep in your game?"

"Uh-huh." He'd climbed as far as he could.

"What do you see?"

"There's a house over there. A white house with a red tiled roof."

"Is it a normal-size house?" I assumed that a Cyclops would have a rather large dwelling.

"Looks normal to me." He went quiet for a moment.

"Tyler, how are we going to find Zeus?"

"Maybe we should go ask the person who lives in that house?" He looked down at me. "Or maybe we should just call Zeus's name. If he's omnipotent, he'll hear us, right?" Before I could answer, Tyler cupped his hands around his mouth and hollered, "Zeus!"

"Hey, I thought you wanted us to be quiet. We sneaked in here, remember?"

"I know but I've changed my mind. Zeus!"

I expected rumbling to fill the sky.

"HEY! ZEUS!" Then Tyler gasped. And pointed.

A woman had appeared at the edge of the field. Her long red hair blew gently in the breeze, as did her long white dress. She was looking straight at us.

"Who's that?" I asked.

"How am I supposed to know?" Tyler scrambled down the tree and jumped into the grass next to me.

The woman began walking toward us. It was a long distance to cross but it must have been some sort of optical illusion because she reached us in three steps. Her gaze settled on the leather bag that was still slung over my shoulder. "Where did you get that?" she asked.

The first thing that struck me was her voice. It was soft and comforting. I didn't know who she was but I instantly felt that I could trust her. But was this some kind of trick? I remembered the story of the Sirens. They sang so beautifully that sailors would forget themselves and try to steer their ships to get closer to the singing. Enchanted by the song, the sailors would steer into dangerous waters and end up dashed to their deaths against the rocks. Was she a Siren?

But the second thing that struck me was her face. She looked exactly like Pyrrha, only older.

"Are you Pandora?" Tyler asked. She nodded. "Wow," he said with a goofy grin. "Uh, hi. I'm Tyler Hoche and this is my brother Ethan Hoche. I'm a friend of your daughter's. Well, we might be more than friends. That's up for discussion. But Pyrrha gave us this bag so we could come through the portal."

"Pyrrha is well?" she asked, her eyes widening.

"Yeah, she's fine," Tyler said.

Pandora's hand flew to her mouth and she gasped softly. Her eyes filled with tears. "I am so happy to hear this news. So happy." Then she looked at the satchel again. "But why did she not accompany you?"

"She's with her dad."

Pandora frowned. Her body stiffened. "She's with Epimetheus? That is distressing news."

Tyler shuffled in place. "Yeah, Ricardo's not our favorite person either. I mean Epimetheus. He has two names so it's kinda confusing. One name for your world and the other name for our world. He probably chose it because Epimetheus isn't a common name back home. I bet most people couldn't even pronounce it." Tyler was rambling. He seemed overwhelmed. I guess for him, this was like meeting a rock star. I thought about speaking up but talking to strangers isn't one of my strengths. The whole eye-contact thing makes me super nervous. Tyler kept talking. "Maybe Pyrrha shouldn't have gotten into his limo but she's trying to help our cousin, Jax. Ricardo kidnapped her. I mean Epimetheus kidnapped her. Jax, that is. Not your daughter. He's trying to take over our world. He's . . . Hey, do you know where we can find Zeus?"

"Why do you seek Zeus?" she asked.

"We need to see him right away," Tyler said. "We need to talk to him."

"That is not advised," she said. Then she stepped closer and lowered her voice. "Seeing Zeus would be to your detriment. Mortals are not allowed in our realm. If Zeus finds you, he will punish you."

Tyler and I looked at each other. Pyrrha had failed to tell us that important piece of information. Beads of nervous sweat broke out along the back of my neck, only to be whisked away by the breeze.

"But Pyrrha told us to come here. Why would she tell us to come here if we're not allowed?" Tyler asked.

"My daughter will do anything to save her father," Pandora said. "Even if it means putting herself and others at risk." She looked over her shoulder. "Come, we must not let Zeus see you. You will be safe in my home. Follow me." She started walking toward the end of the field.

"Wait," I blurted. Pandora turned around. Her gentle eyes settled on me. "If we're not supposed to be here, then I think we should go back through the portal. I think we should leave right now." Zeus had a bad reputation when it came to punishment. I was ready to run back to that tunnel. And I'd set a speed record doing it!

"My daughter needs your help to complete her quest. For her sake, I will keep you safe. And I will assist you in the destruction of . . ." She pointed to the satchel. "The urn of Love."

We hadn't mentioned the urn of Love, but she knew we had it. Had she sensed it, the way Jax had sensed the urn of Hope?

"You can rest assured that I have the same goals as you—to rescue our loved ones and to destroy the urns, once and for all." Then she started walking again.

I wasn't sure what to do. Tyler set his hand on my shoulder. "She's as worried about Pyrrha as we are about Jax. She's promised to help us. Come on, let's go with her."

Despite my trepidation, it seemed the logical

thing to do. But I was being asked to follow a total stranger, to her house, in the Realm of the Gods. We didn't know anything about her, except that she'd opened a famous box that had unleashed evil into the world. Would she really protect us from Zeus? There was no way of knowing.

I hate not knowing.

"Ethan!" Tyler called.

"Yeah, okay." Clutching the bag, I followed.

11
JAX

Ethan would have complained about my lack of a plan. But he wasn't here and I had only myself to rely on. All I knew was that the gate had closed, but the red door might be open. I ran under the archway, past the ticket booth and the welcome sign, and grabbed the red door's handle. Locked! I darted to the gate and grabbed the metal bars. There were no pedestrians on the street. But two of Ricardo's men were still standing on the sidewalk. "Help me," I cried. "Please."

They could hear me. I was only a few yards

away. But they ignored me.

"He kidnapped me," I told them. "Help me."

They stood with their hands at their sides and blank looks on their faces, just like those guards at Buckingham Palace who aren't allowed to talk to people, or smile, or do anything. I tried to shake the gate but it wouldn't budge either. "What's the matter with you? I've been *kidnapped*!" Clearly, they didn't care. "Kidnapping's against the law," I said, trying to threaten them. "If you don't let me go, you'll get arrested. You'll—"

Someone grabbed my shoulder. Instinct took over. I swung around and kicked as hard as I could. It was another man, dressed just like the others. They were beginning to look like clones. He easily avoided my kick. I balled up my fists, ready to punch one of his weak spots, but suddenly, my feet left the ground. Another guy had flung me over his shoulder and was carrying me back toward the limo. "Let me go!" I yelled. I really wished I hadn't quit tae kwon do. I only got to the yellow belt, which is the second belt. What can I say? I got bored. I didn't know that I'd be kidnapped by a crazy mythological man! How could I possibly know something like that? That's not the kind of thing that shows up in a person's horoscope.

"Let me—" I landed on the ground, feetfirst, just like a cat.

The limousine driver stepped forward. "Follow me," he said.

What could I do? Throw a temper tantrum? Sit on the concrete like a toddler and refuse to go? One of the guards would just end up carrying me. There was nowhere to run. And Pyrrha had disappeared. The driver reached out to grab my arm but I yanked it away. "Don't touch me!" I told him. "I can walk without help, thank you very much."

I followed the driver through the double doors, into a long hallway. The place was cold, not the dry kind of cold that comes from air-conditioning, but as if no sunlight ever made it through the thick cement walls. I tried to memorize my steps, in case I needed to backtrack. I kept watch for fire escapes, or windows that might open.

Ricardo had mentioned the driver's name. "Timothy?" I asked, trying to keep my voice calm. "Can't you let me go? I won't tell the police, I promise. You won't get into trouble."

"Where would you go?" he asked in a monotone voice. "You are meant to be here. We are all meant to be here."

The way he spoke creeped me out. Like I was

listening to a robot. He was dressed just like every-one else. Ricardo must have gotten a real good deal on blue suits and sunglasses. "Why are we meant to be here?" I asked.

"To work for the one purpose."

Okay. Creepier by the second. "What is the one purpose?" I asked.

"The one purpose is the only purpose."

I rolled my eyes. *Oh gee thanks, that makes total sense.* Let's try this again. "Uh, Timothy, can you *define* the one purpose? I mean, I know it's the only purpose, but what is it, exactly?"

He didn't answer. I don't know how he could see with those sunglasses. The overhead light-ing was pretty dim. Some of the lightbulbs were buzzing. Maybe the wiring was bad and the place would catch on fire. Then the fire department would come and I'd be rescued.

I decided to try a different question. "How come Ricardo bought this museum?"

"All property is for the one purpose," Timothy said.

"And again, what is the one purpose?"

"The one purpose is the only purpose."

I groaned with frustration. It was like talking to a machine.

We walked down the hallway, passing lots of offices. One of the doors had a sign that read: *Historic Site Research Department*, another: *Personnel Office*. More people, women and men in blue suits and white shirts, sat at the desks, working on computers. The lights of the computer screens glowed on their faces. No one looked up as we walked by. According to a clock it was five a.m. Why were they working so early? What were they doing? "Hey!" I called, rapping my knuckles on one of the doors. But they continued to stare at their screens, as if in a trance.

Were they all victims of Ricardo's urn?

We passed a bin filled with museum brochures. I grabbed one and stuffed it under my shirt. Hopefully there'd be a map inside.

For someone in a trance, Timothy sure walked fast. We passed a woman. She bowed her head at Timothy; he bowed back. "The one purpose," she said to him.

"The one purpose," he said back.

I was putting it together, like a detective. The urn of Faith was definitely at work here. Faith had been stripped from these people, leaving them with nothing or no one to believe in. Then Ricardo had filled that emptiness with himself. He'd become their one purpose. And now they'd follow his commands, even if it meant kidnapping an innocent girl. And he would probably turn the urn on me. I wasn't sure if I was shivering because it was so cold, or because I was really scared. I wrapped my purple jacket as tight as I could. I'd become a follower, just like the other poor victims. I'd start talking about the one purpose.

Ricardo was creating his own cult, except it was powered by magic.

We were in another hallway. This one had a rounded ceiling. White paint was peeling off the walls. One of the overhead lights flickered. I kept going over the route in my mind, so I could backtrack when I escaped.

We came to a circular room. The ceiling was made of metal beams, with lots of rusty pipes running across it. More hallways jutted out of the room, like spokes on a wheel. Each of the hallways had a big number over it. I peered out a narrow window. It was still dark outside, but the first rays of dawn were just beginning to appear. Most of the corridors looked empty, but hallway five was lined with racks of blue suits and white shirts. Timothy turned and walked down hallway four.

We passed lots of doors. Then he opened one. I looked inside. It was a jail cell. No doubt about it. There was only one tiny window and it was set too high in the wall to reach. There was a cot with a blanket, a toilet in the corner, and a sink. A loaf of bread, a jug of water, and an apple sat on a little table. "You will wait here," Timothy said.

"Why?" I could see my reflection in his glasses. I wondered if his eyes looked like robot eyes.

"It is the leader's command that you sleep here. Do you not serve the one purpose?"

If I admitted that I didn't serve the one purpose, would Timothy haul me down to the brainwashing room? It seemed best to pretend. "Yes, I serve the one purpose." I bowed. He returned my bow. Then I stepped into the room and Timothy closed the door. His footsteps echoed as he walked away.

A terrible feeling welled in my chest and I couldn't catch my breath. I'd seen Ethan have anxiety attacks, so I knew what was happening to me. He got them in crowds. But this was the opposite of a crowd. The walls felt like they were closing in. I sat on the cot and gave myself the same advice I always gave Ethan—breathe slowly. Focus all your thoughts on your breathing. Slowly.

Slowly. The feeling will pass.

And it did pass. Fear switched to anger. Stupid Ricardo!

It occurred to me that, at that very moment, my father might be sitting on his cot, looking at the walls of his jail cell. He was there because of Ricardo. Well, the villain wasn't going to imprison me, too. I remembered his threat—*If your cousins do as I have instructed, you will be free to go at eight a.m. If not, then I have other plans for you*. He was going to kill me, a mere mortal. Or turn me into one of his brainwashed robots, working for the one purpose. No way!

Come on, Jax, you can figure this out!

I walked around the cell and checked every nook and cranny. There was shampoo, soap, and two towels. A roll of toilet paper.

And there was the bread.

I was starving. The loaf was small, but crusty and white. It could be poisoned but why would he want to kill me already? He needed me to make the trade with Ethan and Tyler. It could be drugged, to make me fall asleep so I wouldn't be any trouble. But he still needed me for the trade, which was less than ten hours away.

What was I thinking? I knew there'd be no trade. The urn of Hope had been returned to Zeus and destroyed. And even if the boys had found Love, I wouldn't let them give it to Ricardo. I needed to stay alert. I needed fuel. So I took a small nibble of bread, then waited to see what happened. Nothing. I took a larger bite, then waited again. I felt fine. So I ate the entire loaf. I couldn't help myself. I'd never felt so hungry in my life.

The room was so cold it went right through my jacket. I wrapped the blanket around my shoulders, then sat on the cot and read the brochure. It said that Eastern State was the world's first true penitentiary. It said that the building was designed to inspire penitence. I wasn't totally sure what that meant. Where was Ethan when I needed him?

According to the brochure, the cells had held many of America's most notorious criminals, including bank robber "Slick Willie" Sutton and "Scarface" Al Capone. Whoever wrote the brochure described the prison as a haunting world of crumbling cellblocks and surprisingly eerie beauty.

"Beauty?" I said with a snort. The haunting part was probably true. There was even a special ghost tour you could take to visit the haunted cells.

Obviously this brochure had been written before Ricardo bought the place. That's why the sign on the sidewalk had said *Closed for Repairs*. Ricardo didn't want tourists walking through his lair. I looked around nervously. Then I turned to the back page and found a map. I retraced my steps from the main entrance and the offices we'd passed. Then to the circular room, which was called the surveillance hub. There was a dining hall, a basketball court, and a movie theater. There was a death row and a famous escape tunnel, but it had been filled in a long time ago so it wouldn't do me any good. The entire prison was surrounded by the stone wall. The only exit appeared to be the gateway we'd driven through.

This was totally different from the prison where my dad was being held—a minimum-security facility known as a prison "camp." The inmates hadn't committed violent crimes—mostly financial crimes—so they wore nice clothes, got hot meals, had a library, access to email . . .

Email?

I pushed the blanket aside and began to pace, trying to work my thoughts into something. Anything. The window was too high to reach. The door was the only way out. Maybe I could break the lock like they always do in the movies. But I didn't have a bobby pin or anything sharp. I crouched in front of the door and examined the lock. It looked like the kind that a long key would fit into. I grabbed the knob. Maybe if I pushed hard enough . . . ?

The door opened.

Whoa! How was that possible? I'd assumed that Timothy had locked me in but this whole time it hadn't been locked? Then again, why would he lock the door? If I served the one purpose, there was no reason to think I'd want to escape. Timothy had treated me as if I were just another brain-washed zombie. That had been his big fat mistake.

Oh, I had *one purpose*, but it wasn't about helping Ricardo.

I was going to get back to those offices and use one of the computers.

12
ETHAN

FACT: *One of the first things you practice in social-skills class is eye contact. Even though it's very uncomfortable for many people, it's one of the most important forms of nonverbal communication. Too little makes the other person feel like you're not paying attention. Too much, however, can be aggressive and make the other person uncomfortable. Avoiding eye contact in a crowd maintains your individual privacy, which is what I tend to do.*

My teacher likes to say that eye contact is

important because the eyes are the windows to the soul. If that is true, then Pandora's soul was beautiful.

"Welcome to my home," she told us, her eyes twinkling. I couldn't look away. It wasn't because I'd suddenly lost my shyness and had a surge of social confidence. It was because her eyes were mesmerizing. They were almond-shaped and they changed colors. Literally. From blue to green to violet and back to blue. It was distracting.

She opened her front door and led us into her house.

I wasn't sure what to expect, since I'd never been to a god's house before. Technically, Pandora wasn't a god, but she lived with them, which made her immortal. I expected she'd have a mansion or a castle. But the house was small and simple. Like a cottage.

The stone walls and marble floor were white and perfectly polished. The wooden furniture was sparse but elegant. One wall was covered with a dolphin mural, built from colorful mosaic tiles. Another wall had a life-size mural of an olive tree. The whole place was clean, with absolutely no clutter. No stacks of books, or piles of junk mail. No shoes lying around, no coats draped across benches. It was a house without *stuff*. My mom always complains that we have too much stuff and that if she could get back the hours she's spent putting our stuff away, she'd be young again. She'd like this house.

As Pandora walked us through the various rooms, I got a better view of her. Her red hair hung all the way to her waist and it sparkled like her daughter's. Her white gown was sleeveless, and the belt was woven from golden thread. Her skin was very brown, which seemed unusual for a redhead. I wanted to point out that an excessive amount of tanning wasn't healthy, but then again, if you're immortal, you probably don't have to worry about skin cancer. Her feet were bare. I guess she didn't have to worry about stubbing her toes, either.

"I'm wondering about something," I said. "Why did you tell us that we'd be safe here in your house? I mean, is this house magical or something? How can it keep Zeus from finding us?"

"There is no magic in my home," she said. "Only the gods have magic. But Zeus knows he is not welcome here. Thus, he never visits."

Pandora stopped walking and gestured at a wall

that was covered in smaller mosaics. "These are portraits of my daughter," she explained. The first showed a baby with a happy grin. The others caught important moments, like first tooth, first steps. It reminded me of the upstairs hallway in our house where Mom displayed our school photos, even the ones with braces and embarrassing haircuts. I wondered if Pyrrha was embarrassed by any of these pictures. "I miss her," Pandora said. There was so much sadness in her voice that I suddenly felt sad, too.

"She's okay," I told her, even though I wasn't sure that was true.

"Hey, I was wondering . . ." Tyler pushed his messy hair from his eyes. "Is this guy Pyrrha's boyfriend?" He pointed to a mosaic that showed a teenage Pyrrha standing with a young man. He had his arm around her.

"That is not Pyrrha," Pandora corrected. "That is myself and my husband when we were first married. Pyrrha does not have a boyfriend."

A goofy smile spread across Tyler's face. He'd been acting weird ever since we'd met Pyrrha in the parking lot outside Merlin's Comics. He'd been flirting with her nonstop. I knew exactly what he was thinking. He was imagining that when this was all over, he'd ask Pyrrha on a date. I was about to point out that, from what I'd heard, long-distance relationships were very difficult to maintain, even if the two people lived in the same dimension. And even if they were both mortals. The odds seemed stacked against Tyler. But something else had caught my attention.

It was a mosaic of two young men. Both had black hair, and one was clearly older than the other, taller, with more muscles. He stood with his hands on his hips, smiling proudly, as if a spotlight were shining on him. The younger man stood quietly to the side, watching. Pandora stepped next to me. "That is my husband and his brother, Prometheus," she said.

"Prometheus?" Tyler gasped. "Whoa! That's what he looks like?"

"This mosaic was created a very long time ago," Pandora told us. "But he was once a handsome young man. As was my husband." She pointed to the younger man, the one standing off to the side. "Please understand that Epimetheus was a kind soul once. Gentle. Compassionate. The man you met, named Ricardo, is not the man he used to be."

"What happened?" I asked.

Pandora sighed. "His heart was broken."

"By a girl?" Tyler asked.

"No." Pandora's eyes settled to a muted gray. Then she gazed into the distance, as if she could see the story she was about to tell. "When he was young, Epimetheus spent most of his time with his brother, Prometheus. This was when we lived in your world. Prometheus was fond of humans, and he had many friends among them. One day he decided to give them a gift."

"Fire," Tyler said with a knowing smile.

Pandora nodded. "The gift of fire gave man creative power. It changed the balance of things, and this made Zeus angry. In retaliation, Zeus declared that Prometheus would live out eternity, chained to a rock. During the day, an eagle ate his liver. During the night, the liver healed so it could be eaten again and again."

I'd heard this story, but that's all it had been—a gross, impossible story. But as I watched the tension on Pandora's face, I realized that the story was true.

Pandora continued. "Epimetheus grieved for his brother. He pleaded with Zeus to offer mercy. He petitioned the Mount Olympus council. But Zeus's ruling stood. Epimetheus could not free his brother, but he was determined to help him. So he visited his brother each day, bringing him water laced with poppy to make the pain bearable. When Zeus heard of this compassion, he ordered Epimetheus to cease. But Epimetheus continued, so Zeus created a magical barricade so that no one could pass. Without the poppy water, Prometheus suffered, day after endless day. Epimetheus could do nothing. He began to hate Zeus, and that hatred grew with each sunrise until it became a ferocious, unyielding beast."

I would hate Zeus, too, if he'd tortured my brother, I thought.

"When I married Epimetheus, he tried to hide the fact that he hated Zeus. He tried to live within Zeus's laws and he fooled most of us into believing that he'd forgiven Zeus. But Zeus was still angry with both brothers for their disobediences, so he decided to punish them yet again."

"Oh, that's where the wedding present comes in," Tyler said. "Pandora's box. I mean, *your* box."

Pandora didn't seem to mind that Tyler kept interrupting her. I didn't dare say a word. Her story filled my head with all sorts of images, and I tried to imagine Ricardo as a person who had once been caring and nice. Who'd once loved his brother.

Then I felt a flash of hope. Maybe there was still some kindness inside him. Maybe he wouldn't hurt Jax after all.

"To punish my husband for his disobedience, Zeus gave us a wedding present," Pandora explained. "A lovely box, but we were told to never open it."

"That's like when our parents put gifts under the Christmas tree and tell us not to open them until Christmas morning." Tyler frowned. "I always hate that. So I always open a few. Because how can you resist?"

"Like you, Tyler, I could not resist." Her voice had lost all of its musical qualities. It was clearly a memory that still brought pain. She touched her temple, as if a headache might be starting. "I was young and curious. I wanted to know what was inside."

"And that's when evil was unleashed," I said quietly.

"Yes." She sighed. "Zeus told everyone that I had unleashed evil into the world."

The moment turned awkward. What could you say after that? Unleashing evil was a pretty bad thing to do. It wasn't like she'd opened the box and a mouse got out. Or a plague of locusts. It was *evil*.

Tyler's stomach growled.

"Where are my manners?" she said with a graceful wave of her arm. "This way, please."

We followed Pandora into a dining room where a long wooden table was covered with platters of food:

almonds and salty olives, loaves of crusty bread, cheese curds speckled with herbs, and roasted meat. Pandora washed her hands in a bowl of water, then dried them on a linen towel. Tyler and I did likewise. The water was warm, with flower petals floating in it. Pandora sat in one of the chairs, then she motioned for us to sit.

Tyler threw himself into a chair. "Uh, do we have time for this?" I asked. "What about Jax and Pyrrha?"

"I am just as concerned as you are about your cousin and my daughter," Pandora said. "But there are details we still need to discuss. Besides, heroes cannot undertake quests on empty stomachs."

"You got that right!" Tyler said.

Is that what we were? Heroes? I had more questions, but at that moment, my stomach felt as hollow as a gourd. I *needed* to eat. So I sat next to my brother. After setting the leather bag on my lap and removing my baseball cap, I looked around for a napkin but there wasn't one. And instead of a plate, there was just a small serrated knife. "Those things look good," Tyler said, reaching out and stabbing a fig with his knife. He plucked the fig off the end of the blade and ate it. He then grabbed a whole roasted chicken, tore one of its legs, and bit into the crispy skin.

Pandora didn't cringe at Tyler's manners. It appeared that eating without a fork or plate was acceptable. I tasted one of the figs. Then the bread and cheese curds. The flavors burst in my mouth. I tried not to talk with my mouth full but I couldn't help it. "This is so good!"

Pandora sat quietly, drinking from a silver cup and watching us with curious interest. I felt self-conscious all of a sudden. She was observing me, a human, a mortal. Did we look weird to her because our hair didn't sparkle? Or because our eyes didn't change color?

"Are you thirsty?" she asked. She presented us each with a small bowl. Tyler cupped it in his hands and gulped the contents. I wasn't so sure about drinking the stuff. The liquid was metallic, like melted gold.

"What is this?" I asked.

"Ambrosia," she said.

"Seriously?" Tyler laughed. "I'm drinking ambrosia!"

I took a small sip. It was thick, like honey diluted with water. But it tasted like nothing I'd ever known. Just incredibly delicious.

Tyler started taking pictures with his phone. Then

he leaned sideways and took a selfie with Pandora. She didn't seem interested in the technology. That's when I realized I hadn't seen any televisions or computers in the house. No machinery either. I suppose if you live in a world with magic, you don't need technology. "When we get home, this is going to be my screen saver," Tyler said.

Home. That word brought me back to reality. It was so easy to get distracted by the beauty of this place. I set down my bowl and looked at Pandora. "You said there were more details we needed to discuss."

"Yes." She set aside her drink. "What conditions has my husband set for your cousin's release?"

Tyler wiped his mouth on his sleeve. "Epimetheus wants all three urns. He has the urn of Faith already. But he wants us to deliver Hope and Love to him by tomorrow morning or we'll never see Jax again."

"Those urns," she said, her voice quieting to a hiss. "How I curse those urns."

"What really happened?" I asked. "I mean, we know the story that we've read in books. But what made your husband leave this place? Why is he trying to take over our world?"

She scooted to the edge of her chair and folded her hands on the table. Whatever she was about to tell us, it was important. "During our marriage, Epimetheus's hatred for Zeus continued to grow. But he had one thing that brought him joy and that was our daughter, Pyrrha. He adored her. Her hugs comforted him. Her laughter warmed our home. I thought that her love would heal him. But one day, Zeus sent the urns." Tyler and I leaned closer, to catch every word. "Zeus told the world that the urns were a symbol of his magnificent power. They were for Pyrrha and no one else was allowed to open them or they would be ruined. The urns sat on a mantel in this house and each day, my husband would stare at them, his hatred raging. He wanted to destroy something that was important to Zeus. So he opened all three urns. And as they emptied, so too did my husband's heart empty."

"Zeus knew he'd open the urns," Tyler said. "It was revenge, right?"

Pandora nodded. "Zeus had inflicted another punishment upon the brothers—Epimetheus would live a life without hope, love, or faith. Zeus was finally satisfied. His revenge ended and he allowed Hercules to free Prometheus. But my husband could not be freed. He was forever changed. His heart was broken."

It was a sad story. To think that the man we'd been afraid of, the man who was back home terrifying people, had himself been the victim of a vengeful god.

"That's a terrible thing to do to someone," I said. "Zeus is cruel."

"That he is," a voice bellowed.

Startled, we all turned in our seats. A large man stood beneath the archway. He glistened with sweat, as if he'd walked a long distance. He was bare-chested, wearing a sort of kilt and a leather apron. He carried a giant hammer.

"Why did you summon me?" he snarled at Pandora. "You know I have work to do."

"I summoned you because I need you," she replied with a patient smile. Then she rose to her feet and motioned in Tyler's and my direction. "Tyler Hoche and Ethan Hoche, I am pleased to introduce you to Hephaestus, son of Zeus."

A clunking sound filled the air. I whipped around. Tyler was lying on the floor.

13
JAX

Clutching the map, I stepped cautiously out of the cell. I half expected to hear the ghosts of prisoners past, clanging their metal cups against the bars or dragging chains as they paced their cells. But it was quiet in the hallway. No signs of anyone walking around. No ghosts or brainwashed followers.

If I was going to pull this off, I needed to look like a member of the cult, dedicated to the one purpose. So I hurried to hallway five. The suits were hung neatly, in order of size. I grabbed the smallest pants, suit coat, and shirt I could find, then slipped into a room. I dressed quickly. The suit didn't fit perfectly but it would work. I rolled up the pant hems so they wouldn't drag, and tucked in the shirt. Once the suit coat was buttoned, I felt like a bank teller. *Hello, how may I help you today? Would you like to make a deposit? Perhaps you'd like to deposit your brain for the one purpose?*

There was a bin in the center of the room filled with discarded clothes—jeans, sweatshirts, tennis shoes—regular stuff that Ricardo's followers had worn before being brainwashed. There was more evidence of their past lives: umbrellas, purses, and hats. One of the umbrellas had a name written on its handle—Dagmar Watson. How had Dagmar gotten stuck in this mess? Did her family wonder where she was? Did she have children? I felt so sad looking at the pile of clothing. Each item represented freedom taken away. I didn't add my clothes to the bin because no one was going to take my freedom. I hated leaving my purple jacket behind because it had always been my good-luck jacket, and if there was one thing I could use, it was good luck. I slid my wallet into the back pocket of the blue pantsuit, along with my house key. Then I folded my jeans, shirt, and jacket and tucked them behind a radiator.

One of the walls was lined with shoe boxes, each containing a pair of black dress shoes. I decided to keep my sneakers, since I might need to run. Besides, those dress shoes made loud clicking sounds, and I needed to be as quiet as possible.

I read the brochure map again. Then I stepped into the hallway, and nearly bumped into a woman with short black hair. "The one purpose," she said with a bow.

"The one purpose," I said in my best robot voice. I also bowed.

She walked away. No questions about what I was doing, or who I was. She didn't seem to notice my shoes, or the nervous sweat on my forehead. I sighed with relief. As long as I looked and acted like one of the cult, no one would question me. I had to stay confident. Had to act like I belonged.

I hurried to the hall with the offices. They were still filled with people, sitting at computers. But one office had a single desk, and the man sitting at it was old and bald. His eyes were bloodshot, as if he'd been up all night working. I tiptoed and stood behind him. There was a basket of wallets on the left side of the desk. He'd opened one of the wallets and had spread the contents on the right side. The driver's license photo was of an elderly woman with the name Dagmar Watson. The umbrella owner. The man was reading an email.

FROM: AAA Mortgage Company
TO: The New Mount Olympus
Corporation
SUBJECT: Dagmar Watson Property
We have received the notarized
documents. Ownership of the
property listed at 822 Village
Circle Drive has been transferred
to the New Mount Olympus
Corporation.

I glanced at the pile. The address on Dagmar's driver's license was 822 Village Circle Drive.

That's what Ricardo was doing! After brainwashing his victims, he made them turn over all their possessions. Other than robbing banks, he was robbing individuals. Pure evil genius! But why was he calling his corporation the New Mount Olympus? Did this have something to do with

Mount Olympus, the home of the gods? Of course. He wanted to erase Zeus and become the new god, and this world would become the new Olympus.

I gasped, and when I did, the man turned around. I bowed. "The one purpose," I said.

"The one purpose," he said.

"Uh . . ." How could I get rid of him? I needed that computer. I thought about it for a moment. "Ricardo said it's my turn to sit here. For the one purpose."

He stood immediately. "I live to serve his command." He bowed again, then walked down the hall.

Wow, talk about easy peasy. Luckily I didn't have to type in a password because the man had left the screen open. I plopped onto the chair. The wood was warm. I didn't know how long it would be before the man returned so I had to act quickly. I selected *compose* and a new email screen appeared. Ethan and Tyler knew that I was at Eastern State Penitentiary. They knew that the exchange would take place by eight a.m. But if they were unsuccessful, if Ricardo turned the urn of Faith on them, then no one would know what had happened to us. I had to tell someone. My mom knew nothing about the urns, so she wasn't a good choice. And Great-Aunt Juniper had suffered a stroke, so she didn't need the extra stress. But there was one person who knew all about Great-Aunt Juniper's secrets. About the magical urns. And what we'd been up to.

My father.

When I'd visited him at the Brookville Federal Prison Camp, he'd given me his email address, and I'd tucked it into my wallet for safekeeping.

FROM: Jax Malone
TO: Isaac Romero
SUBJECT: Ricardo

I paused. Were Brookville prison emails private or did they get read by the warden? Maybe it didn't matter either way. If the warden read this email, he'd probably think the sender was crazy and he'd probably ignore the whole thing. I typed as fast as I could, not worried about typos.

Ricardo kidnaped me. I'm at East State Penn museum. He has Faith. He wnts Ethan and Tyler to bring

**Love and Hope 8am tomorrow. I will
try to escap but he might use Faith
against me. If that hapens, tell
Mom the truth. I don't want her to
think that I joined Ricardo. Tell
her I love her.**

Should I have told Isaac that I loved him too?
He was my father, but I didn't know him. I hadn't
even known that he was alive until last month.

I looked around for a phone. There was a land-
line sitting on the corner of the desk. That meant I
couldn't send a text to Tyler, but I could call him. I
picked up the receiver. Then I dialed Tyler's number. It didn't ring. Instead, a recorded voice said,
"Unauthorized call. Please enter your security code
followed by the pound sign." I quickly hung up.

Footsteps echoed down the hall. Drat! I'd been
caught. I returned to the previous screen showing
the email from AAA Mortgage Company. Then I
scooted out of the chair and was ready to bow and
act innocent.

"Jax?" Pyrrha stopped in the doorway. She was
still wearing her blue tunic and sandals. "I've been
looking everywhere for you. What are you doing

in here?" She glanced at my clothes and her face turned pale. "Oh no. Did he . . . ?" She put a hand to her mouth. "Jax? Did he . . . ?"

"It's still me," I said.

Her hand dropped to her side. "Oh, thank the gods. I am so very sorry about all this, Jax. But how did you . . . ? Never mind." She looked up and down the hallway. "My father is distracted. His mind is infected with hubris."

"I don't know what that means," I said with a frown.

"Hubris is excessive self-confidence. It infects the mind like an illness. It is a terrible curse. He believes himself unstoppable. However . . ." She glanced over her shoulder, then whispered at me. "This hubris makes him vulnerable, and that is our advantage."

"So, are you telling me that you're still trying to stop him?" I asked. "You're still on our side?"

"Yes, of course. My quest has not changed. The urns must be destroyed. But I am determined to save my father at the same time." She grabbed my arm. "Come with me." She pulled me into the hall.

"Where are we going?" We weren't walking toward the front gate. I'd imagined myself busting through that red door. Or calmly telling the guards to let me out because Ricardo had ordered me to get him a latte at the nearest Starbucks, for the one purpose.

"Father sent me to get you. We're supposed to wait in the auditorium for the ceremony."

"What ceremony?"

"He has invited dignitaries from all over the city to take part in a grand reopening ceremony for the museum."

"What?" I yanked my arm from her grip. "No way," I said. "I'm not going to some super boring ceremony. I'm getting out of here."

"But you don't understand—"

"Oh, I understand. I understand everything. Your father isn't just taking control of people's minds, Pyrrha. He's taking all their belongings. Their bank accounts, their houses. He's using the urn to make himself super rich. He wants to be the most powerful man in the world."

"In my realm, magic brings power," she said.

"Well here, money is power. And he's getting a lot of it. I have to find my cousins. If they do show up, I have to get to them before Ricardo does."

"I have a better plan," she said.

14
ETHAN

FACT: *Fainting is a sudden loss of consciousness. There are a lot of reasons why a person might faint—a sudden drop in blood pressure, physical trauma, or the emotional shock caused by coming face-to face-with a real, living god.*

As far as I knew, Tyler had never fainted. He'd lost consciousness when he was exposed to the urn of Hope, but that was totally different from fainting. If we'd been in our world, I probably would have called 911, or insisted he go see a doctor. But under the circumstances, I wasn't worried. The only reason I hadn't fainted too was because Tyler's fall onto the stone floor had distracted me.

He was only out for a second. "You okay?" I asked, helping him sit up. Pandora also rushed to his side. She held a cup of cool water to his lips. He drank a few sips.

"What happened?" he murmured as he rubbed his shoulder, which had taken most of the impact.

"Forgive us," Pandora said in her lilting voice. "We forget that you humans are delicate creatures. We did not mean to frighten you."

"Huh?" Tyler looked very confused. Then a large, oil-stained hand reached out. Tyler looked up and when he saw Hephaestus staring down at him, all the color drained from his face. I thought he might pass out again!

"Go on, boy, get up," the god said brusquely.

Tyler just sat there, frozen in place. Hephaestus grabbed Tyler's hand and yanked him to his feet. "Uh . . . th . . . th . . . thanks," Tyler mumbled.

Hephaestus grunted some sort of response. Then he limped to the far end of the table. He didn't wince as he limped, so it wasn't a twisted ankle. I vaguely remembered that he'd been born deformed, but I couldn't quite recall the whole story. Tyler would know, and I was really curious. But I'd learned in social skills class that if someone is physically different, it's best to let that person bring up the subject.

The god set his hammer onto the table, then sat in a chair. Pandora took her seat and, once again, motioned for us to sit. Tyler was a bit wobbly on his feet so I pushed him onto his chair. Then I also sat. We turned and stared down the table at the new guest.

It might sound mean to say this, but it's the truth—Hephaestus was ugly. His nose was crooked and swollen. One of his eyes only opened halfway because of a thick scar that covered the eyelid. His black hair was long and greasy, and his beard was matted. His posture was hunched and there was a hump on his back. It didn't make sense that a god would suffer from osteoporosis and a limp. If he had magic, why didn't he cure himself?

"I can't believe I'm meeting you," Tyler said, finding his voice again. "You're the god of blacksmiths, sculptors, artists, fire, metals, and volcanoes. You make all the weapons for the gods, and you also made Hermes's helmet and sandals, Achilles's armor, Helios's chariot, and Eros's bow and arrows." I wasn't sure why Tyler was giving Hephaestus a description of his own deeds. I guess he was nervous. Tyler suddenly stiffened. "Hey, is it true you use Cyclopses in your forge? As your assistants?"

Hephaestus cast an annoyed glance at Tyler. He mumbled some comment about Cyclopses being lazy. Then he grabbed a platter of fish. They were small, but cooked whole, with skin and eyeballs still attached. He held one of the fish by its tail and bit off its head. I did my best not to gag as I thought about what it would be like to bite into eyeballs. We sat in silence, watching him eat. Well, it wasn't exactly silent, because he chewed with his mouth open, and he smacked his lips. Fish scales got stuck in his black beard. There were so many things I wanted to ask, but I had enough trouble talking to strangers, let alone talking to *a god*. Any conversations I'd had with a god had been those few times I'd gone to church and we'd knelt to pray. Even though I'd never seen any physical proof that God exists, I still went through the motions, just in case. But in those situations, no God ever replied. Or *appeared*.

Pandora smiled at me. She'd noticed that I was squirming nervously. She gently nodded and I knew that I needed to be patient. He would speak when he was ready. And when Tyler opened his mouth, she put a finger to her lips.

So we waited. I was excited *and* terrified. The most amazing thing was happening to me at that very moment. On the other hand, this god, who was the son of Zeus, had overheard me say that I thought Zeus was cruel. I'd said that out loud! I didn't know he was standing behind me. But as he'd stepped into the dining room, he'd said that he agreed with me. At least, I think that's what he'd said. I couldn't be certain. My heart was pounding so hard I started to worry that it might burst. I really wanted to google "bursting hearts," to see if that was possible.

Hephaestus finished all the fish and two more platters of food. He tossed bones over his shoulder and didn't bother to wipe crumbs off his leather apron. He took a long drink of ambrosia. His belch echoed off the stone walls. Then he sat back in his chair, stretched out his legs, and began picking at his teeth with one of Pandora's knives.

"Why are two humans in our realm?" he asked. His voice was not smooth or lilting like Pandora's. It was gruff and sounded as if he'd swallowed gravel. "This is a direct violation of Zeus's laws."

I cringed. Every minute Tyler and I sat at that table

was another minute when Zeus might discover us.

"They are here," Pandora told him, "because Pyrrha sent them here. She needs our help."

At the mention of Pyrrha's name, Hephaestus stopped picking his teeth. His eyes widened. "Pyrrha? She is still in the mortal world?"

"Yes," Pandora said.

Outside the window, a rumbling sound arose. "What's that?" I asked, nearly jumping out of my chair.

"My father is holding the council meeting on Mount Olympus," Hephaestus said. He grumbled something under his breath. Then he scratched his beard with his blackened fingers. "They spend their idle lives arguing about trivial issues, while the rest of us toil to keep them happy." His tone was clearly resentful. "Why did Pyrrha send mortals?"

I looked at Tyler. He was the leader of this quest, so he should be the one to answer. "Out of curiosity," Tyler said, "how can you tell we are mortals?"

Hephaestus narrowed his good eye. "How do you tell a blade of grass from an oak tree?" I guessed that this was a rhetorical question. He was letting us know that we were insignificant beings. He smacked his hand on the table and the platters vibrated. "I do not like to be kept waiting. Why did Pyrrha send mortals? If she needs help, she should come to me herself." He got to his feet. "Enough of this. I have a helmet to repair."

"Sit down," Pandora urged. "Listen to their story."

With a frustrated grunt, he sat. I didn't want to keep a god waiting so I elbowed Tyler. He cleared his throat and started to explain. "Epimetheus has the urn of Faith and he has some sort of plan to take over our world. He's willing to hurt anyone who gets in his way. He kidnapped our cousin, Jax, and unless we bring him the urns of Love and Hope, we will never see her again. But we know that the urns must be destroyed. So we came here, to give the urn of Love to Zeus so that he can destroy it, just like he destroyed the urn of Hope when Pyrrha brought it back."

"You say Zeus destroyed Hope?" Hephaestus asked. "That is not possible."

"We saw her carry it through the portal." I finally found the courage to meet his gaze. "She took it to Zeus."

Hephaestus looked down the table at Pandora. I got the feeling that they knew something we didn't.

"What's going on?" Tyler asked. "Please tell us."

Pandora frowned. "I am sorry to say, my daughter lied to you."

"What?" Tyler looked heartbroken. "She . . . *lied*?"

"The urns cannot be destroyed individually. They were forged together and thus, must be destroyed together," Pandora told us. Then she rose from her chair, left the room, and returned a moment later with an urn in her hand. I recognized it immediately. It was a small clay jar, black, with white swirls painted all over it.

Tyler recoiled. "Get that thing away from me," he said through clenched teeth.

"No harm will come to you," Pandora assured him as she set it onto the table. Tyler scooted his chair back, his eyes darting as if he was looking for an escape. Even though I'd seen the urn's powers, I didn't feel as afraid as Tyler. Pandora had no reason to open the urn. We were not her enemies. We were her only link to her daughter.

"Why doesn't Zeus have it?" I asked.

"Pyrrha brought the urn home but she never spoke to Zeus," Pandora said.

"Why?"

"It is forbidden for us to travel to your world. Pyrrha went without Zeus's permission. If he finds out that she broke his law, he will require some sort of retribution." Tears welled in the corners of her eyes. "He has long tormented my family. He must not discover that Pyrrha has broken his law."

"That means we can't ask for his help," I said. This realization hit me like ice water.

"You came here to seek help from my father?" Hephaestus laughed, but it was not joyful. It was a tragic kind of laugh. "Foolishness."

"You do not need Zeus's help," Pandora said. "Hephaestus is the one who forged the urns. He has the power to destroy them. That is why I summoned him."

Hephaestus took another swig of ambrosia, then wiped his mouth with the back of his hand. "I am far too busy to deal with matters of the mortal world," he said gruffly.

"Listen to me!" Pandora cried. Anger flashed across her face. Her eyes turned fiery. "You will help these mortals!"

Was she actually giving orders to a god? Was this going to get dangerous? Where was the nearest exit?

Hephaestus rose to his feet. He began breathing very quickly and his face went red. Steam drifted from his ears and nose. The entire room turned hot all of a sudden. I wanted to run, but I sat glued to my chair. "You dare tell me what to do?" he bellowed.

Pandora bravely stood her ground at the opposite end of the table. "I know you do not care if my husband lives or dies in the mortal world. But I speak the truth when I say that you bear some responsibility for the tragedy that has befallen my family. And now you have the opportunity to set things right."

His long greasy hair hung across his face, but I could see that he was staring at her with his one good eye. The steam disappeared, but he didn't say anything.

Pandora softened her voice. "Please, Hephaestus. Please make things right. You loved me once, long ago. If you won't do it for me, do it for Pyrrha. She has always cared for you."

Tyler's mouth was wide open. This was like watching a soap opera. Hephaestus had loved her. She'd rejected him. But now she needed him. We waited for his response. I had no idea what was about to happen.

He grunted. Then he pushed the hair from his eyes. "You speak the truth," he finally said. "I am partially responsible. I was distracted by drink when Prometheus stole fire from my forge. That stupid oaf.

What a lot of trouble he has caused."

The sound of thunder rumbled again in the distance. Hephaestus looked out the window. "I will help these mortals."

I was sitting in a chair, at a table. And then, I wasn't.

In the span of a heartbeat, without warning, the room turned black and then I was standing on a ledge, looking down into a huge cave. Tyler was standing next to me. I wasn't sure what had happened. Or where we were. But what I knew was that Tyler was squeezing my arm real hard. "Is that . . ." He gasped. "Is that a Cyclops?"

15
JAX

Pyrrha and I both bowed as two women walked past. They wore equally dazed expressions on their faces. Guess that's what happens when you've had your brain erased. "The one purpose," we all said. As soon as they'd turned a corner, Pyrrha opened a door and we stepped outside.

Morning had arrived. The temperature was already warming. We were standing between two long buildings—more spokes on the wheel that was the design of this weird place. There was some noise in the distance. Some of the followers were carrying flowers and balloons. "What's going on?" I asked.

"It's for the reopening ceremony."

"Oh, right. Wait, why would he reopen this museum? Why would he want tourists walking around?"

"He is not going to reopen it," she said. "But the guests do not know that. They believe they have been invited to attend a grand ceremony of significant importance. They are influential people—wealthy museum donors, foreign dignitaries, even the mayor and chief of police are coming. My father will use this event to increase his power."

Of course. The guests would gather in one room, Ricardo would open the urn and voilà—instant minions. With a mayor and chief of police under his influence, he'd quickly take over Philadelphia. Then move on to the next city, and the next. He'd amass wealth, destroy all traces of Zeus, and set up his New Mount Olympus.

Pyrrha took my hand. "If you still want to escape, I will take you to the entry gate and set you free."

That was a tempting offer. To be free. To catch a bus home to Chatham and hug my mom and sit in my backyard and never think of Ricardo again. But for how long? I knew the truth. So did Tyler and Ethan. Ricardo would come after us.

"I'm not going anywhere."

"Are you certain?"

"No," I said. "I'm not certain. And don't ask me that again because if I think about it, I mean, *really* think about it, I'll probably change my mind. So, what is the plan?"

"Before you agree to help me, I need to tell you something." She ducked into a shadowy alcove. No one was around. Pyrrha stood real close to me. She still smelled like peeled oranges and mint, just like the first time I met her. I could practically count the freckles on her nose. She was so pretty, with her long glittery red hair. And her perfectly tan skin that looked really nice against her blue tunic. I thought her eyes were brown, but now they seemed violet. Were they changing colors? "There is much you do not know."

"What don't I know?" If I'd asked Ethan that question, he would have recited all sorts of facts to me. His long answers usually bored me. But I missed him so much, I even missed his factoids.

"After you disabled the security system in the

Museum of Fine Arts, Ethan found the urn of Love. He carried it out of the museum."

"That's the best news I've heard in a long time." I smiled. Great-Aunt Juniper would be proud. So would my dad. But Pyrrha wasn't smiling.

"When we left the museum, I was going to take the urn of Love back to my realm. But my father kidnapped you and that changed everything. So I told Tyler to deliver the urn. I gave him the key to the portal."

"Whoa!" I said. "Are you kidding? Tyler's in the Realm of the Gods?"

"I cannot be certain, but I expect he followed my directions."

"Of course he followed your directions," I said. "You could tell Tyler to jump off a bridge and he would. Well, maybe that's going too far but he'd do mostly anything for you. He has a huge crush on you." Had I said too much? She didn't look surprised. She'd have to be blind not to have noticed the way he looked at her.

This latest news was almost unbelievable. My geeky cousin who'd been creating a game based on the world of the gods had gone into *their world*. "Then that means the urn of Hope *and* the urn of

Love have been destroyed," I said. "That's even better news." Except it meant the boys wouldn't be able to trade those urns for me, which kinda sucked.

Pyrrha's frown deepened. "They have not been destroyed."

"What?" I didn't understand. "But you said—"

A small group of followers walked past. They were carrying more decorations for the fake ceremony. We all bowed and declared our commitment to the one purpose. I don't think any of them actually looked at my face. I was just another blue suit I guess. As soon as they'd entered the building, Pyrrha continued. "I told you the urn of Hope had been destroyed. But in truth, I took it home and left it with my mother. The urns cannot be destroyed individually. They were created together, and so they must be destroyed together."

"Wait . . ." I shuffled in place. "You lied to us?"

"I did not want to burden you with the details."

I'd have to remember that excuse the next time my mom caught me in a lie. Sorry, Mom, but I didn't want to *burden you* with the details.

"The urns will be destroyed, Jax, that is no lie. I took the urn of Hope to my home for safekeeping.

Once I have all three, I will ask Hephaestus to destroy them. And then I will beg Zeus, once again, to forgive my father."

I couldn't remember who this Hephaestus guy was, but I didn't care. None of these Greek names were easy to pronounce and I was super worried about my situation. Ricardo would be pissed when he found out that my cousins had nothing to trade. And he would probably turn that anger on me. "Okay, so the urn of Hope and the urn of Love are at your mom's house. All we have to do is get the last urn." It sounded easy but I knew it would be the most dangerous and difficult thing I'd ever done.

"Yes." She furrowed her brow, as if she had a headache. "Jax, there is something else. I am afraid I made a terrible mistake."

"I'm listening," I said, dreading whatever was about to come out of her mouth.

"I gave Tyler the key to the portal but I was in such a hurry I forgot to warn him." She began chewing on her lower lip.

"Warn him about what?"

"Mortals are not allowed in my world. If Zeus finds out . . ." Tears filled her eyes. "Oh, Jax, my father hurt your family by sending your father to prison. And now I have sent your cousin into a dangerous situation. I am so very ashamed." She began to cry.

I didn't know what to say. I felt real hot all of a sudden. Anger filled my entire body. Those stupid gods and their stupid magic! If Zeus hurt my cousin, I'd volunteer to help Ricardo destroy all the Zeus statues! I'd be the first in line to help wipe Zeus off our planet! But then I took a deep breath and listened to Pyrrha as she tried to explain.

"My . . ." She choked on the word. "My father was changed by the urns but once they are destroyed, the power they have over him will also be destroyed. He will be my father again. And I will have my family back. We will be together. It's what I've wanted for such a long time. But in wanting this, I may have gone too far."

It was an honest explanation. She wanted her fairy-tale ending. What would I do to have my family back? How far would I go to have my mother and father still married, living happily ever after? It was a nice image, even though I'd never lived it. "Look, here's what I think," I said. "Tyler is super smart. He can take care of himself. Even if you'd warned him about Zeus's laws, I think he still would have gone through that portal. He takes the whole hero-on-a-quest thing very seriously." Was Tyler okay? We didn't know, so it was best to focus on what we did know. I was in deep trouble. Without Hope and Love, Ricardo would not be setting me free. He had *other plans* for me. And whether I ran away, at that moment, back to Chatham, he'd still find me. This had to end! "We need to find the last urn. Where is it?"

She wiped away her tears. "It is nearby," she said. "I can sense it." Then she hugged me. "I was so scared when I saw you dressed like the others. I am so glad you are not changed. I will make this right, Jax. I will. I promise."

"*We* will make this right," I told her. "Together."

16
ETHAN

FACT: *In our world, there is a genus of copepods (small crustaceans) that live and function with one eye. This creature had been aptly named Cyclops. However, we humans are designed with two eyes. This is mostly a function of symmetry, which tends to be a default setting in our DNA. A person with one eye can see distance as well as a person with two. But the slight advantage to having two eyes is that they expand close-up vision, allowing us to see both to the right and to the left. This makes us better at judging depth.*

Which probably explains why the mythological Cyclopses seemed so clumsy.

There were eight of them. They were big guys, at least ten feet tall. I didn't notice any females in the group, but I'm not familiar with Cyclopsean biology so I could have been mistaken. They were gray-skinned, as if they'd never stepped out into sunlight. I guess that's what happens if you live in a cave. The texture of the skin was rough, like stone. I thought that they might benefit from a good loofah, to help shed some layers. Their heads were hairless, and their foreheads broad, the single eye placed in the center. Like Hephaestus, the Cyclopses wore leather aprons. Two of them held enormous pickaxes and were cleaving boulders from a section of cave wall. The other six were carrying the boulders to a large pool of bubbling liquid. It looked like molten metal.

The clumsiness came in their inability to walk back and forth from the pool without bumping into each other. That led to lots of hollering in a language that was mostly grunts and growls. One Cyclops swung his massive arm and smacked another Cyclops in the ear. That led to the other Cyclops dropping his boulder on the first Cyclops's foot. If this had been a movie, the scene might have been comical. But my entire body was trembling!

Tyler stared with his mouth wide open. He'd been doing that a lot since our arrival. I might have done the same thing but I didn't want to inhale any weird stuff that could set off my allergies.

We stood on a ledge above the cave, looking down at the working Cyclopses. There was no safety railing and I was struck by a wave of vertigo. One wrong move could send us falling into the pool. I stepped back and bumped into a wall.

"OMG," Tyler whispered. "They have yellow blood. That's awesome. I'm gonna change that in the game."

Tyler's observation appeared to be true because a yellowish goo was oozing out of the Cyclops's foot, right where the boulder had landed. The injured Cyclops roared with anger, then picked up the same boulder and tossed it at his coworker. His aim was horrid, however, because the boulder soared right over his intended victim's head, toward the ledge. Our ledge.

"Duck!" Tyler cried, pulling me down. The boulder whizzed overhead and broke to pieces on the cave wall behind us. Luckily, we were untouched. Physically untouched. But emotionally, I was a wreck. My heart pounded and my nose started to tingle. Crud! I yanked one of my ever-present tissues from my pocket and held it to my right nostril as blood began to trickle.

"Let's get out of here," I insisted, my voice somewhat muffled by the tissue.

"What?" Tyler looked at me as if I belonged in a psychiatric hospital. "Why would I leave? Dude, we're looking at Cyclopses!" While I was trying to keep from totally freaking out, Tyler stood up, took out his phone, and held it up for a photo. I think it was too dark in there for an adequate shot, but I didn't say anything. A flash of light went off, illuminating the cave. The Cyclopses stopped working. They blinked, as if dazed. Then they turned. The camera had sensed the lowlight conditions and had automatically employed the flash. "Uh-oh," Tyler said.

For a moment, the cave fell into silence.

Then the Cyclopses dropped their pickaxes and boulders and lumbered across the cave, pushing, shoving, and tripping over each other as they headed toward our ledge.

Toward us!

Tyler turned. "Okay, now's a good time to leave. RUN!" he screamed. But there was nowhere to run, what with the wall behind us and a steep drop on either side. Tyler and I pushed our backs against the wall, then he flung his arm across my chest, the way my mom always did when she had to stop suddenly while driving. When the Cyclopses reached the ledge, we could only see them from the neck up. Eight huge gray heads. Eight curious eyes. One of them began to drool. Another licked his crusty lips. Why were they making unmistakable "yum yum" sounds?

"Do not eat the mortals!" a voice bellowed.

Hephaestus, son of Zeus, was somewhere in the cave, though we could not see him. A bell chimed. The Cyclopses blinked a few more times, then turned and began to lumber away. They disappeared down a tunnel.

As soon as they were gone, Tyler exhaled. "That happened, right? That actually happened!" He was talking so fast, spit flew out of his mouth. "Up close and personal. Wow! I can't believe it. They were looking right at us! They don't have eyelashes. Did you notice that? And their nostrils quivered when they smelled us. Like rabbit noses." He seemed delighted.

"They were going to eat us," I told him, just in case he'd missed that fact.

"I can't believe it," he said again. "That was the best moment of my life!"

"A thank-you would suffice!" the voice said, followed by a grunt.

Tyler and I took a few steps and peered over the ledge. Hephaestus stood beside the molten pool, the urn of Hope in one hand. "You two were almost Cyclops fodder."

I gulped. "Thank you."

"Yeah, thanks." Tyler shoved his phone into his pocket. "Where's Pandora?"

"She is not needed here. I only brought you two."

"What is this place?" I asked.

"Welcome to my palace," Hephaestus said, his gruff voice dripping with sarcasm.

I didn't see any furniture. Or personal items of any sort. Perhaps that stuff was in a different section of that cave. "Why did the Cyclopses leave when the bell rang?" I asked.

"Break time," Hephaestus explained. "They need to be fed thirty times a day or they won't work. They barely work as it is. You would think the son of Zeus could get a better class of laborers, but the only creatures who work down here do so because they are shunned aboveground." I guessed he was referring to his own grotesque appearance, as well as the Cyclopses'. He put his hands on his hips. "Why are you still on that ledge?"

I pressed the tissue harder against my nostril. "Is there a way down?" I asked.

Hephaestus glared up at us. "I forget. You are mortals." He waved an arm and suddenly we found ourselves standing next to him.

Heat radiated from the pool. Bubbles rose to the surface, then popped and splattered. Up close it looked like metallic silver paint. Tyler was about to dip his finger in. "If you cherish the use of your hand, I would not do that," Hephaestus said calmly.

Tyler yanked his hand away. As a gamer, his hands were everything. "What is it?" he asked.

"The source of all I create." Hephaestus grabbed one of the boulders, then tossed it into the pool. The rock began to melt. "This is the metal of the gods."

"Whoa," Tyler said. "Awesome. So this is where you made Eros's arrows? And Hermes's winged sandals?" Hephaestus nodded.

"And the urns?" I asked.

Hephaestus nodded again, then pointed at my face. "What ails you?"

I could feel my cheeks go red. "Uh, you mean my

nose?" He grunted. "It's a stress reaction. When I get nervous, my nose starts to bleed. Not all the time, but some of the time. It's . . . embarrassing."

"Embarrassing?" He scratched his tangled beard. "Am I correct to assume that mortal females do not like bleeding noses?"

"Not so much," I said.

"Do they find your bleeding nose abhorrent?"

"Yeah, some of them do," I admitted, remembering all those times in school when the sudden spray of blood had caused a commotion. I didn't mention that the real reason I had only one female friend, and she was my cousin, was because of my social anxiety.

"Girls aren't super crazy about gaming geeks, either," Tyler said with a shrug.

Hephaestus nodded. "Females also find me abhorrent."

Though I appreciated this sort of bonding, I thought "abhorrent" was a bit of an exaggeration, at least as far as Tyler and I were concerned. While we weren't princes of eloquence or social butterflies, we weren't *ugly*. Tyler could use some basic lessons in hygiene, but so could most of his friends.

"Females," Hephaestus said with his trademark grunt. "Difficult to exist with them, difficult to exist without them." He cleared his throat, then spat into the pool. Then he scratched *other* parts of his body. He wasn't such a bad guy, I realized. Not half as scary as those Cyclopses. My nose had stopped tingling. I wadded up the tissue and stuck it into my pocket.

Hephaestus began to limp slowly around the pool and toward a fire that burned in a stone hearth. We followed. "This is where I formed the urns," he explained, pointing to his forge. He set the urn of Hope on a workbench. "Zeus commanded me to build them. I did not know he would use them to torment Pandora's family. Had I known my father's intent, I would have refused him. But he does not forgive easily. If he is fond of you, your days will be blessed. But if you disappoint . . ." He stared at the fire with his good eye, as if lost in memory.

"Did he really throw you off a cliff when you were a baby?" Tyler asked. "That's what the stories claim."

"When he saw my *deformities*, he cast me off the mountain."

"That's terrible!" I blurted.

"Terrible?" Hephaestus snorted. "That is the way of the gods! I survived. The only permanent damage was to my foot. I manage to get around."

The image of a baby being thrown off a mountain

was horrific. He'd obviously survived, physically, but what about the emotional damage? Did he have a counselor to talk to? A support group? That kind of trauma would leave deep scars.

Talk about a dysfunctional family of epic proportions.

An uncomfortable silence loomed. I remembered Jax and our mission. "So, if I understand this correctly, you made the three urns here, so this is where they need to be destroyed?"

"Correct," he said. "But they must be destroyed together."

I opened the leather bag and handed him the urn of Love. He set it beside the urn of Hope. They made a pretty set, something you might see on a grandmother's mantel. "We don't know how to get the third urn," I told him. "Epimetheus still has it. He kidnapped Jax and told us that if we don't bring him Hope and Love by eight a.m. tomorrow morning, we will never see Jax again." Each time I repeated Ricardo's threat, it was like a knife to my stomach.

"And Pyrrha?" Hephaestus asked. "What of her?"

"She's with her father right now," Tyler said. "We think she's trying to convince him to come home."

"She is risking her life to save her father," Hephaestus said. "She must believe that if the urns are destroyed, they will no longer have power over him. And his soul will heal. He will love his family again."

"Will he?" I asked.

"Perhaps," he said. "But even though I was once married to Aphrodite, goddess of love, I am no expert in matters of the heart." He suddenly looked pained, as if he'd been struck by a migraine. While I'd never heard about him being tossed off a cliff, I remembered that marriage part of his story. His union with the most beautiful goddess on Olympus had not worked out. While he'd adored her, she hadn't returned the feelings.

But enough about theses gods. Jax was waiting for rescue. My thoughts spun round and round. The situation seemed hopeless. "What are we going to do?"

Tyler rubbed the back of his neck. Then his brow furrowed. "If we try to get the third urn from Epimetheus, chances are he'll open it and we won't know what hit us. We'll become his zombies." His arms dropped to his sides. "OMG, what if he's already opened it in front of Jax and Pyrrha?" Had this thought just occurred to him? Had he been so distracted by the Realm of the Gods that he hadn't considered this? I'd been worrying about it nonstop.

"It would appear you have only one choice," Hephaestus said. "You must deliver the two urns to Epimetheus as he demanded."

"Huh?" Tyler said. "But—"

Hephaestus shot Tyler a stern look. Tyler swallowed his objection. "As I was saying, in order to rescue your cousin and ensure Pyrrha's safety, you must deliver the urns. If you can get all three urns together, in one place, they can be destroyed before Epimetheus has the chance to use them."

"How can we destroy them?" I asked.

"With fire," he replied.

"But Great-Aunt Juniper tried to destroy them with fire and they wouldn't burn," Tyler said.

"You must use a special flame. My flame." He reached his hand into his forge. I winced, but the god showed no sign of pain. When he pulled his hand out, a small orange flame danced in the center of his palm.

"Wow," I said.

"The fire that formed the urns is the only fire that can destroy them." He stepped close to Tyler. Even though Hephaestus was hunched over, he towered above my brother. "Hold out your hand." Tyler obeyed. Hephaestus grabbed Tyler's left hand, which looked like a baby's hand compared to the god's. He pressed their palms together. "Tyler Hoche, elder brother of Ethan Hoche, I hereby bequeath you with the sacred fire born from the forge of Hephaestus, son of Zeus." He lowered his hand. Tyler gasped. The thin orange flame was now dancing on Tyler's palm.

"Wow," Tyler said. Even though fire was touching his skin, Tyler didn't appear to be in pain. He closed and opened his palm. The flame was gone. He closed and opened it again; the flame was back. It was a trick any magician might master, but this was no illusion. It was real, godly magic.

"Touch that flame to the urns and they will burn, but only if they are together," Hephaestus instructed.

At least we knew how to destroy the urns, but we still had the problem of getting the third urn from Ricardo. "Uh, I'm still wondering—"

A shuffling sound arose. I darted around. "They're coming back," I said with alarm. The Cyclopses must have finished their meal because they were lumbering down the tunnel. A couple of them were gnawing on large bones. One still had a napkin tucked into his leather apron. Another one belched and the scent of sulfur filled the cave.

"Time to return you to Pandora," Hephaestus said. He raised his arms. Was he going to transport us again? I hoped so. Those Cyclopses were getting closer.

"It was very nice to meet you," I said. Then I grabbed the urns and shoved them into the leather bag.

"Hang on." Tyler took out his phone again. "Can I take a photo with you?" Without waiting for the god's permission, Tyler squeezed next to him, held up the phone, grinned, and snapped a selfie. "Awesome!" The flash caught the Cyclopses' attention. They dropped their bones and picked up speed. Even though they'd just eaten, they still looked hungry.

"Uh, I think we'd better go," I said, clutching the bag to my chest.

"But I still have so many questions," Tyler said. "I'm developing a game called Cyclopsville and—" One of the Cyclopses picked up a boulder and took aim.

"Could you get us out of here?" I pleaded.

"Good luck with your quest, boys," Hephaestus said. "And good luck with the females!"

Tyler aimed his phone at the Cyclopses but I'm not sure if he got a picture or not because, once again, I felt the ground disappear under my feet and even though everything went dark, I knew we'd left the cave.

17

JAX

Pyrrha had the ability to sense the urn's location, so as we walked along a pathway, she was like a bloodhound following a scent. We stopped at the front door of a building, between blocks five and six. I checked my handy map. According to the brochure, this building had once been the prison chapel, but was now used for museum events.

One of Ricardo's followers set a sandwich board in front of the building. *Grand Reopening Ceremony*, it read. An arrow pointed to the front door. More followers were coming and going, bringing in chairs, platters of food, stuff like that. My ugly blue suit was really coming in handy. No one paid any attention to me. A few bowed, but most were too busy. Pyrrha still looked like a Greek goddess in her embroidered tunic and sandals, but no one seemed to notice her, either. They were all focused on their jobs.

It seemed weird that Ricardo was letting Pyrrha walk around unsupervised. He totally trusted her. Or else he was testing her. Or maybe she was right. He was overconfident. That *hubris* thing she'd mentioned. He thought he could do no wrong. He thought he had everything figured out.

Well, not with Jax Malone around!

I followed Pyrrha inside. Flowers and balloons decorated the corners of the room. There were tables set up with pastries, coffee, and tea. I guess it's polite to serve your guests a light breakfast before attacking them with a brainwashing urn. Pyrrha looked around, then pointed up the stairs. We waited for two women to pass us. They were carrying folding chairs. Then we went upstairs.

The chapel was a small room with white walls and wooden beams that ran across the arched ceiling. There were no pews, but I imagined the prisoners, long ago, who'd sat in that place, praying for freedom. The two women had joined three others and were setting up the folding chairs in tidy rows, facing the chapel's altar, which looked like a little stage. A banner hung across the stage: *New Mount Olympus Corporation*. A mountain with a snowy cap was the company logo.

Pyrrha stopped walking. "Is it here?" I quietly asked her. Then I noticed what she was looking at.

A white pedestal stood in the center of the stage. It looked like a column from an ancient Greek temple. A large, golden mask was perched on top of the pedestal. The mask was a man's face but it looked more cartoonish than real. His ears were small and roundish. His eyes were closed and his nose was long and thin. He was smiling, as if dreaming about something nice. Four men stood on the stage, two on each side of the mask. Even though they were dressed like everyone else, I could tell they were security guards because they wore earpieces and stood ready to draw their guns if necessary. Though I couldn't see their eyes through the dark glasses, they seemed to be staring straight ahead. That mask must have been super important. "What is it?" I whispered to Pyrrha.

She turned to me and frowned. "That is the Mask of Agamemnon."

What? I gasped. My father was in prison because he supposedly stole the Mask of Agamemnon. But there it was, in Ricardo's lair. I clenched my fists. Not only had Ricardo set up my father, he'd kept the stolen mask for himself. I wanted to scream. Wanted to punch Ricardo. Wanted to make him hurt as much as he'd hurt my family!

Pyrrha leaned close. "The urn is here," she told me. "It must be behind the mask." She climbed onto the stage. A guard immediately stepped forward.

"No one is allowed on the altar," he told her in a monotone voice.

"But I am Pyrrha, daughter of Epimetheus." She paused. "Daughter of Ricardo. He has given me permission to approach the mask."

"No one is allowed on the altar," the man repeated. Another guard grabbed Pyrrha's arm and *escorted* her off the stage.

When the guards had returned to their places, Pyrrha casually walked back to me. "The urn of Faith is definitely behind the mask. I saw it," she whispered.

A tingle ran up my spine. It was so close. We could grab the urn and run down the stairs and out the red door. But how could we get past those men? They were beefy, that's for sure. The seams in their blue suits were practically ripping from their muscles. Had Ricardo recruited followers at a weight-lifting competition?

I looked around to make sure no one was paying attention to us. "Why this mask?" I asked. "What's so important about it?" Once again, I needed Ethan's factoid brain. Had he gone into the Realm of the Gods with Tyler, or had he stayed behind? Was he okay?

Pyrrha's voice was so quiet I could barely hear her above the sounds of chairs being unfolded. "Agamemnon was a very important king. A conqueror. My father admired him."

I wanted to tell Ricardo that no matter how many people he brainwashed and controlled, no one in this world would ever really, truly admire him! "How can we get the urn?" I asked. "Maybe we can distract those guys?"

"Yes, a distraction." Pyrrha's eyes sparkled. "When we were in the Museum of Fine Arts, I caused a distraction by pretending to be sick. It worked."

I didn't need directions. I'd been in a few plays at school. With a huge groan, I clutched my stomach. "Oh, I'm sick. Something's wrong." The guards didn't flinch. "Help!" I fell to the floor. The guards didn't even look at me. But one of the women who'd been setting up the chairs walked over. She knelt.

"Do you require medical attention?"

"No," I said, getting to my feet. What was the point of pretending to be sick if the guards wouldn't budge?

"The one purpose," she said.

"Yeah, yeah. The one purpose." I straightened my suit coat. The woman went back to setting up chairs. "Now what do we do?"

Pyrrha's expression turned stormy. "We have come so far. We are so close to finishing the quest," she said between clenched teeth. "These mortals will not tell me what to do." Then she let out a huge, angry breath. With stomping steps, she climbed back onto the stage. "Move aside," she ordered in a loud voice. "For I am the daughter of Ricardo and he has instructed me to deliver the urn." Even though the guards loomed over her, she stood her ground.

One of the guards spoke. "Our orders are—"

"You dare to disobey Ricardo?" She pointed at him. "I am his daughter, and the one purpose is my purpose. Are you against the one purpose?" Emotion appeared on the guard's zombie face. He was confused.

"The one purpose," he said with a bow. Then he stepped aside. But the others did not. Pyrrha raised her voice even louder. "I said that I am Ricardo's daughter and he has ordered you to let me pass!"

I scrambled onto the stage. I knew that if I touched the urn of Faith, I would feel its warmth, and it would get into my head. I would become its protector. I didn't want any more urns talking to me, controlling me. But this had to be over. I lunged for it. A guard blocked me. I bounced off him and stumbled backward. Pyrrha darted around the mask, her arms reaching. But a guard grabbed her around the waist. She threw a punch, knocking him on the shoulder. Then she broke away and did a roundhouse kick, right in his gut! He actually flinched. I wondered what kind of martial arts they taught in her world. Sign me up!

But the guards outnumbered us. They backed us into a corner of the stage. "I told you," Pyrrha said, trying to catch her breath. "Ricardo ordered me to get the urn."

"He has ordered no such thing," a familiar voice said.

The guards stepped aside. Ricardo stood in the chapel's doorway. His fedora cast a shadow over his face but from the tone of his voice, I knew his eyes were burning with rage.

He slowly walked into the room, past the rows of chairs, until he stood at the base of the stage. "It is most disappointing that you failed my test," he told Pyrrha. "Like your mother, you cannot be trusted. Seize her!"

Two of the guards grabbed Pyrrha by her arms. "RUN!" she yelled at me. But it was too late. I was in their clutches. And Ricardo was pointing at me.

"Soon," he said, "you will join the others. You will exist only for the one purpose."

18
ETHAN

FACT: *Transporting from one place to another place by means of magic causes dizziness and confusion. It can also be life-threatening, especially if you are being transported into a cave of flesh-eating Cyclopses. But once you rematerialize, and get your bearings, the dizziness passes. If you find yourself in the Realm of the Gods, however, you may still feel confused. It's a very confusing place.*

We were standing in a field of lavender. The scent of warm fruit filled my nostrils, which was so much nicer than the sulfuric stench of Cyclops burps. We'd left Hephaestus's forge and were back in Pandora's field. We needed to get home. We needed to destroy the urns and save Jax. The leather bag was in my arm, Tyler was a couple feet away. The trees were still heavy with ripe apricots, but something had changed. The sky wasn't robin's egg blue. The sun wasn't shining. Thick gray clouds churned and thunder clapped. "Pandora!" a voice bellowed. "What have you done?" The words shook the ground like an earthquake.

Zeus.

Pandora ran toward us, her dress rippling in the wind. "He comes," she called, her eyes wide with alarm. "Hurry!"

Wasn't he supposed to be in a meeting on Mount Olympus? I started running. So did Tyler. Through the fear, I tried to pull my thoughts together. We needed to get to the portal. We needed to avoid Zeus. We needed to get back to our world. Like in a nightmare, my legs felt rubbery. Was I moving in slow motion? Why was it so difficult to run? Was it fear or some kind of magical spell?

A bolt of lightning illuminated the distant mountain range. Another bolt hit a nearby tree. A branch shattered.

"Tyler!" I cried. Tyler darted out of the way. A chunk barely missed him as it fell.

We'd almost reached the edge of the field where the terrain changed from grasses to rocky outcroppings. A series of stone hills ringed the edge. One had an opening. The portal's tunnel.

"Pandora!" Zeus's voice shook the ground again. I cringed. Did he always sound that angry? What would happen if he caught us? Mortals were not allowed in this world. Pandora had taken us to her home, had fed us, and had helped us. For our sakes as well as hers, we had to make it to that tunnel.

The wind began to howl, pushing against us as if trying to keep us from leaving. Pandora's hair whipped in rope-like strands. Another lightning bolt struck, cracking a tree in half. This was worrisome. Trees are natural lightning rods, but so are people. While it was possible to survive being struck by lightning, I really didn't want to add that to my résumé.

And then we reached it. I almost cried with relief. Pandora pointed to the leather bag. The golden trident was glowing. "You must protect this key. Do not let my husband have it. It is Pyrrha's only way home."

"I will protect it," I told her.

"Tell Pyrrha that I love her. Tell her to return to

me." Her beautiful eyes filled with tears.

"We will," Tyler said. "But, you know, I was kind of hoping that she might hang out a bit longer. I'd like to show her around. Take her to a—"

"Tyler!" I said.

"Yeah, yeah, I get it. But what about Zeus?" he asked Pandora. "Will you be okay?"

"Hephaestus will distract him with a shiny new helmet. Do not worry." Then she hugged Tyler and me. She smelled like ambrosia.

"Thank you," he told her. "This has been the best freakin' day of my life!"

"Thanks," I said with a quick wave. There was no time for ceremony, or the exchange of phone numbers. Maybe I could send a thank-you card later.

Then, with Zeus's bellowing voice filling the heavens, we ran into the tunnel.

19
TYLER

Welcome back to the Game.

You are logged in as Tyler. You are seventeen years old. Energy levels are at maximum thanks to food and ambrosia supplied by Pandora.

Your teammate is Ethan, your younger brother. He is thirteen years old and recently suffered a nosebleed brought on by an overactive nervous system.

Status: You are mid-transport, between your world and the Realm of the Gods.

Possessions: Your phone, a leather bag, the urn of Love, and the urn of Hope. You also possess a secret weapon, hidden in the palm of your hand.

Your objectives: Unite the three urns, destroy them, save Jax, save Pyrrha, and end Ricardo's villainous reign.

And win the immortal girl's love and affection.

Restart Game.

20
ETHAN

FACT: *We stink under pressure.*

Normal sweat is meant to cool us off, but stress sweat causes cortisol and adrenaline to rush into the bloodstream, making you go from zero to sweaty in seconds flat. When you sweat, you feed the bacteria that naturally live on your skin. Their digestion produces the odor we call BO. While exercise sweat is mostly water, stress sweat has a lot of fat and protein so the bacteria love it and make a lot more odor.

Tyler reeked. But so did I. That was the first thing I noticed after our transportation. I'm not sure why. It would make more sense for me to notice that we were standing in a new location. But we'd gotten a bit jostled during transport through the Poseidon Portal and I ended up with my nose pressed against Tyler's back. Good thing my nosebleed had stopped back in Hephaestus's cave.

"We're not in the park," Tyler said.

I stepped away. I'd expected we'd be back in Boston Common, standing in the fountain, but we were somewhere else. I felt stunned, looking around for any clues to our whereabouts. We stood on a sidewalk lined with brick buildings. Each had apartments on top and shops on street level. But the sidewalk across the street was lined with a tall stone wall. A tower rose in the distance. It looked like a medieval fortress.

Tyler whipped out his phone, checking the map app. "Philly," he said. "We're in Philly. Outside Eastern State Penitentiary."

"The gods sent us to Jax," I said with a gasp.

"And to Epimetheus," Tyler said. "They saved us five hours of driving."

I grabbed his phone and read the screen. We were

two blocks from the penitentiary's entrance. "How are we going to get our car?" I asked. "It's back in Boston."

"Who cares?" Tyler said, snatching his phone back. "We can deal with that after Ricardo has been *vanquished*." He said this with a burst of energy, waving his arm as if brandishing a sword. "Come on."

As usual, he took the lead, without any discussion. "Tyler," I said, stopping him by grabbing his sleeve. "We should make a plan. We can't just barge in."

"You can't always have a plan, Ethan. Believe me. I've fought enough battles to know that most of the time you have to think on your feet." He was talking about virtual battles, of course.

"But—"

I expected to be dismissed, to be put in my place with some comment reminding me of his genius status. But instead, he put a hand on my shoulder. "Okay, I'm listening. What do you suggest?" His voice was tight with impatience, but he was asking for my opinion. This was a huge change in our relationship.

"I think . . ." Like the heroes in the games he played, Tyler was eager to venture forth and engage in whatever battle awaited us. In those games Tyler always won. But this was no game and I needed to remain the voice of reason. "I think Jax might still have my phone. Should we try to text her?"

He thought about this for a moment. "Too risky. If Ricardo took it, then we'd be alerting him to our location." He scratched his face. The stubble was filling in. If he went without a razor for another day, he'd have a full beard. Would this quest take another day? Would we ever get back home, where things like shampoo, clean clothes, and razors waited for us? Along with parents.

Tyler turned around. The shop behind us was a coffeehouse. The scent of freshly ground beans wafted from the open door. There were two customers, drinking from mugs and reading the newspaper. "You take the urns and wait in there," he said, giving me a nudge.

"What?"

"Ricardo wanted to meet by eight a.m., right?" I nodded. "It's 7:50. I'll go. I'll tell him that he can have the urns *after* he sets Jax free. No urns unless she is free." That sounded good. "Once she's out of his grip, I'll stick her in a cab and get her out of the city. She can start heading home." He looked at the leather bag. Then he looked at me. "I want you to go with her."

"But—"

"I'm not going to argue about this, Ethan. As soon as Jax and you are in the cab, I'll take the leather bag and deal with Ricardo."

"Alone?"

"Yes." He started to pace. "I assume Ricardo will bring the urn of Faith with him when he meets me. It's his best weapon in case I try to run. If he has the urn of Faith that will mean that all three urns are in the same place. I'll set the leather bag on fire and try to reach Faith, too."

I looked at his palm. "Do you still have it?"

Tyler opened his palm. The little flame flicked like a cat's tail. He closed it again.

There was no doubt in my mind that I wanted to climb into a cab with Jax and get as far away from Ricardo and this nightmare as possible. But leaving Tyler alone was not an option. He'd already taken a huge hit when the urn of Hope had been unleashed. I couldn't let that happen again. I looked down the street, toward the penitentiary's entrance. I was going to insist that we walk there, together, but something was wrong.

"Why are those guys running?" I asked, my entire body stiffening. Tyler followed my gaze. Two guys, dressed in blue suits and wearing dark glasses, had crossed the street and were heading toward us. Maybe they were out for a morning jog, or were anxious to get their lattes at the coffeehouse behind us, but I doubted it. They looked like CIA agents.

"RUN!" Tyler shouted.

It was just as difficult to run down the sidewalk as it had been to run through the field with the godly wind blowing against me. My legs were weak and wobbly. I wondered if this was a side effect from traveling to another realm. When astronauts return to Earth, they suffer from muscle deterioration. Had that happened to me? Or, after all the excitement, had my fight-or-flight mechanism been overworked, leaving me weak and easy prey? Tyler raced ahead but didn't make it beyond the next intersection. Two more men had darted around the corner and were blocking his way. They were dressed like the others. Tyler skidded to a stop. I caught up with him. We were both breathing hard. "What do you want?" Tyler demanded as the first two men stood guard a few yards away.

"Come with us. Ricardo is waiting for you," one of them replied.

"We're not going anywhere," Tyler told him. "Not

until Ricardo releases our cousin, Jax. And not until I watch Jax and Ethan get into a cab."

"Ricardo is waiting for you," the man repeated. His voice was robotic.

Would it do any good to cry for help? What would happen? A few pedestrians might gather. The police might come. And then Ricardo would unleash one of the urns and we'd all be captive. The only chance humanity had was for us to get all three urns in one place.

"We'll go with you," I told the thugs. Tyler glared at me. But his anger was a brief flash, quickly extinguished by truth. He knew we had to go. He knew what we had to do.

One of the men tapped his earpiece. "We have them," he said.

We walked with our escorts to the museum's entrance. The entry was cut into the stone wall and blocked by a metal gate. A pair of gargoyles sat on the edge of the wall. They looked clean and new, as if they were recent additions. Their eyes flashed red. Security cameras, I realized. Another pair of guards stood beside a red door.

Cabs and limousines pulled up to the curb. People had begun to gather outside the museum. Most of them were dressed nicely, as if they were going to an important meeting. A woman in a blue suit and dark glasses began to address the crowd. "Tickets for the grand reopening ceremony are required. Please form an orderly line. The ceremony will begin soon." Her voice was as unemotional as our escort's voice. I knew, without a doubt, that the blue suits were under Ricardo's spell. The urn of Faith had turned them into mindless followers.

"Excuse me," a young woman said. She was speaking to the blue-suited woman. "I'm the mayor's chief of staff. I think the mayor would be more comfortable inside, rather than waiting in line. Would you please let us through?"

"All guests must wait here," the blue suit replied. "Ricardo is not yet ready. The grand ceremony will begin soon."

Ricardo had invited the mayor and all these people to some kind of ceremony? Should I warn them? Tell them there had been a bomb threat and that they shouldn't go inside? Tyler had already been escorted through the red door. I was only a few steps behind when a car came to a screeching stop in the middle of the road. It was a blue BMW like the one my father drove. The passenger door flung open and a woman with brown hair stepped out. "Jax!" she cried. It was my aunt Lindsay, Jax's mom. Then my dad got out of the driver's seat. This was unbelievable. How had they known where to find us?

"Da—"

It was too late to warn them because a bunch of blue suits swarmed me and, like being caught in a current, I was whisked through the red door.

Once I got inside, a hand was placed over my mouth and I was forced past a ticket booth and into a courtyard. Neither my dad nor Aunt Lindsay had seen me. If Jax were in this situation, she'd probably bite her captor's hand, but I did no such thing. I didn't want to risk being separated from Tyler. We needed each other. Ricardo had abandoned his family. Madness might have been the cause of his actions. But even if I went crazy, even if Ricardo exposed me to all three urns, I'd never abandon Tyler or Jax.

Never!

I was released from the man's tight grip. Tyler and I stood next to each other. We were somewhere on the museum grounds, the giant stone wall separating us from the outside world. There was no sign of Ricardo. Or Jax. Or Pyrrha. Sweat broke out along my shirt collar. Would we ever emerge from this place?

"Inside," a woman said. Her hair was pulled into a tight ponytail. I could see my reflection in her sunglasses as she pointed to a building. A banner across the entrance read: *Grand Reopening Ceremony*. Two balloon bouquets stood on either side of the door. It was odd to see such a happy symbol in such a dark place. When I was little, I loved balloons, and like most kids, I cried if my balloon floated away. Until that very moment I never realized why. To a young child who doesn't understand the laws of physics, a balloon seems like a magical thing and when it floats away, so does the magic. But I was no longer a little kid and I knew that the balloons were filled with helium. And the only kind of magic waiting inside that building was the kind that emptied the soul of the things that make life worth living.

Tyler glanced at me from the corner of his eye and held up his fist, in a gesture of solidarity. The flame waited beneath his curled fingers. I clutched the leather bag and we entered the building and headed upstairs.

My nose didn't tingle.

The blue suits led us into a room that looked like a small church. Rows of chairs faced a little stage. There were flowers and streamers, as if a wedding was going to take place. But I didn't notice much more because Jax was standing on the stage, her arms behind her back. She was being held by one of Ricardo's followers. Pyrrha was also being held. They both gasped when they saw us.

And I gasped too, because Jax was wearing one of the blue suits. Had she been brainwashed?

"Tyler, Ethan, run!" Pyrrha cried. But even if we'd wanted to, there was no escape. Our escorts stood, blocking the door.

"Jax, are you okay?" I cried.

"It's behind the mask," she said. Her voice was not robotic. She kicked the man who was holding her but he simply gripped her tighter. She was still her old self, which was great news, but equally great news was that the third urn was here, in the room. My heart beat so quickly it felt like it was in my throat. The urn of Faith was on that stage, behind the mask. We were so close. We could do this!

"Well, well, it would appear we have a family reunion in progress," Ricardo said, his voice sounding as ominous as it had over Tyler's phone. He stood in the center of the stage. Morning sun streamed in through the narrow windows, casting odd shadows on his face. Before this moment, I'd only seen him at the comic-book festival, when he'd been chasing us. He wore a black suit and black fedora. His face was narrow, but handsome. His eyes were dark and piercing. I shivered.

His gaze lingered on the leather bag. "You have brought the urns," he said. It was not a question. I realized he could sense their presence.

"You said if we brought them, you'd let Jax go," Tyler told him. Tyler reached into the leather bag and pulled out the urn of Hope. Then he stepped in front of me. "Let Jax, Pyrrha, *and* Ethan leave this place, now, or I'll open this urn."

I took a sharp breath. It was a brilliant strategy, which didn't surprise me. Tyler was thinking on his feet, just like he said. We knew that the urn of Hope left everyone in a semi-comatose state. If Tyler opened it, he would be safe because he held the urn. Pyrrha and Ricardo would be safe because the urns couldn't hurt them. But everyone else in the room would be affected, including me and Jax. Ricardo would have no brainwashed followers to protect him, making it much easier for Tyler to get the third urn.

Ricardo stood his ground, his eyes never blinking. "Your threat is empty," he said with certainty. "You will not open Hope."

"What makes you think that?" Tyler asked, clutching the urn.

"Because you know what it feels like to have hope drained from your soul. You would never expose your brother to such suffering."

I chewed on my lip as I tried to read Ricardo's expression. Did he remember that he'd once loved his own brother? That he'd tried to help ease Prometheus's suffering? But I saw no flicker of emotion. His voice remained icy.

"Let them go," Tyler demanded, his hand gripping the urn's cork.

"Go ahead," Ricardo said. "Open it."

They stood, facing each other from across the room, one daring the other to hurt his brother and his cousin. If Tyler opened the urn, I wouldn't question his decision. I would forgive him. "Go ahead," I said. "Do it!"

"Open it!" Jax cried. "Don't worry about us! You have to stop him!"

But Tyler didn't make a move. A smug grin of satisfaction stretched across Ricardo's face. "Just as I expected. Love has clouded your judgment. It has made you weak." Still standing on the stage, he took two steps backward. "It is time for you, Ethan,

Tyler, and Jacqueline to serve me as I create the new Olympus on Earth. My one purpose is now your purpose." He reached behind the mask and lifted an urn. The third urn. It was the largest of the three and pure white.

"No, Father, please!" Pyrrha cried. She squirmed, trying to get free. "Do not do this. I beg of you."

I was surprised that he'd acted so quickly. I guess I'd expected a villain's speech, something grandiose and insane. That always happens in the movies. But as soon as Ricardo had grabbed the urn of Faith, he uncorked it.

We'd failed.

21
JAX

It was happening. Really happening. Ricardo was opening the urn of Faith.

My knees went weak. I felt sick to my stomach. I knew what was about to be unleashed. Upon Ethan. Tyler. Me. We were going to be zombified, just like rest of the brainwashed followers. Mindless servants. Soulless robots. Tyler would never finish designing Cyclopsville. Ethan would stop sharing his factoids. And I'd never ride my bike again. Or lie in bed and read my travel books. Or eat breakfast with my mom at the Chatham Diner. I'd stop being Jax.

"Run!" I told my cousins. I tried to twist out of the blue suit's grip but couldn't. "Run!" But Ethan and Tyler didn't run. They didn't try to fight their way past the two guys who guarded the door. They just stood there, watching Ricardo. Ethan looked terrified as he stared at the urn in Ricardo's hand, but he didn't leave Tyler's side. And Tyler, well, he didn't look scared. He didn't even flinch. Half his mouth curled in a weird smile.

"Bring it on," he said like a superhero in a movie.

My mouth fell open. *Bring it on?* Tyler had been attacked by the urn of Hope, but there he was, smiling as the urn of Faith was opened. And there was Ethan, standing perfectly still, not trying to escape. There was only one explanation.

My cousins knew something I didn't know.

Silence filled the chapel as Ricardo extended his arms, holding the white urn for all to see. A whooshing sound emerged from its opening, quiet at first, then getting louder the way a train does when it comes down the track. The wind came next, rising from the urn in a single rope-like strand. The strand rose toward the ceiling, slithering like a snake. Then it split, forming three branches. I craned my neck, watching as the branches halted, then pointed at their victims. Not the blue suits, for they'd already been attacked. Not Pyrrha or Ricardo. One branch pointed at Tyler, one at Ethan, and one at me. And then, like snakes on the attack, they slithered toward us. The wind got stronger. Ricardo's fedora blew off his head. Wind whipped through my hair and stung my face as the magic came closer and closer. It would reach inside me and take all my faith. It would change me. Control me. "Tyler!" I cried. "Do something!"

Even though I yelled at him, I didn't know what he was supposed to do. He was holding the urn of Hope in his right hand. What would happen if two urns were opened in the same room? Would the building collapse from that much wind and magic? Would a giant sinkhole form or a mushroom cloud like you see in those old atomic bomb films?

Would we survive?

"Father!" Pyrrha cried. "It is not too late. Stop. Please." I could barely hear her above the howling.

Tears filled my eyes. The slithering wind was only a few inches away. My bones felt cold, like I'd been dipped in ice. Everything I believed in would be taken from me. What did I believe? I believed that Ethan and I would always be best friends and that we would grow up and do amazing things. I believed that it didn't matter if you were a gamer geek, a science nerd, or a girl who liked to read travel guides, we all deserved to choose our destinies. And I believed that my family was the most important thing: my mom, my cousins, my aunt, uncle, and great-aunt, and even though I didn't know him very well, my dad.

The tendrils were about to touch us, when Tyler reached out his left hand. A flash of orange caught my eye. A flame flickered on Tyler's palm. He was holding fire. How was that possible?

Ricardo had also noticed the flame. His voice broke through the wind. "NO!"

Tyler reached up and touched the magical tendril that had been coming straight for him. The tendril ignited and the fire spread, as if following a trail of gunpowder until it reached the urn of Faith. The wind disappeared and the urn erupted in Ricardo's hands. With a cry of pain, Ricardo dropped Faith onto the stage, then staggered backward, knocking the golden mask off its pedestal as flames engulfed the urn. The fire grew larger, like a beach bonfire.

The man who'd been holding me let go. I was free. Pyrrha was free too. The guys who were standing at the door looked dazed, as if they'd been sleepwalking and had woken up in a place they didn't know. Ricardo's face glowed as the flames danced in front of him. His eyes flashed red. "Hephaestus!" he cried, clenching his burned hands.

"Now!" Tyler told Ethan. Tyler lunged forward and tossed the urn of Hope into the fire. The flames doubled in size. The stage itself caught fire and smoke began to fill the air. Ethan opened the leather bag and pulled out a small red urn. I guessed it was the urn of Love.

A strangled sound came out of Ricardo's mouth, not a word but a cry of agony. Pyrrha tried to grab his arm, but she wasn't quick enough. Ricardo leaped off the stage and landed on Ethan. They both fell to the floor.

Tyler and Ethan were trying to destroy the urns and the fire was the way to do it! I raced around the flames and jumped off the stage. Smoke stung my eyes. The blue suits seemed wide-awake now, no longer robots, because they hurried out the door, abandoning their former leader as they tried to escape the smoke and flames. Tyler was on top of Ricardo, trying to pry him free of Ethan. Everyone was yelling. Ethan wanted help. Pyrrha wanted her father to stop. Tyler wanted Ricardo to leave Ethan alone. But no one was paying any attention to the little red urn that had rolled into the middle of the aisle.

I grabbed it.

And threw it into the fire.

The explosion was like a firecracker, the kind I hate because they don't make pretty colors, just a big loud bang. Flames rose to the ceiling. Streamers melted. Wooden beams caught fire. The New Mount Olympus banner turned black and disintegrated into floating pieces of ash. There was so much smoke I couldn't breathe. I started coughing.

"Yes!" Tyler yelled. "We did it!" He started coughing too. The smoke filled the space until I couldn't see Ethan, or anybody. I heard sounds of shuffling, heavy footsteps, more coughing. A low moaning sound might have been Ricardo, but I couldn't be sure.

"Keep low!" Ethan cried. "Smoke rises. Crawl toward the door!"

I knew he was right. We'd practiced this emergency drill in our school back in Chatham. I fell onto my knees, bumping into chairs as I inched my way up the aisle. Tyler called Pyrrha's name.

Smoke billowed out the door, as if it also wanted to escape the inferno. Once I got through the doorway, I turned to find Tyler and Pyrrha crawling out. We scrambled to our feet and stumbled down the stairs. We made it outside, but the fresh air didn't help my coughing, or my stinging eyes. There were about a dozen people in blue suits standing around. "Where am I?" one of them asked. "These aren't my clothes," another said. A few were crying.

"Where's Ethan?" Tyler asked. I spun around. The staircase was empty. Why wasn't he with us?

"Ethan," I said, still not able to take a full breath. "Ethan."

"My father," Pyrrha said. Her face was covered in soot and her dress was singed.

"Stay here," Tyler told us. "I'll go get them."

"I'll go," Pyrrha said. "I am immortal. The fire will burn me, but I'll survive."

"No!" Tyler blocked her with his hand. "You are not going back in there. Stay here with Jax. She needs you." Then he ran back into the smoke. I leaned against a wall. Even though I wanted to help, there was no way I could follow Tyler. My lungs were burning. Pyrrha watched Tyler run back up the stairs, her hands clenched worriedly at her sides.

"Tyler," she whispered.

I'd never coughed so hard in my life. My head felt like it might explode. My knees gave out and I sank onto the ground. Pyrrha knelt beside me. "Jax, what can I do? How can I help you?"

Ethan. Please be okay. Please be okay.

And then he ran out of the building, smoke billowing behind him. His baseball cap was gone. But he carried two things. The leather bag and a golden mask.

"Jax," he said, falling to his knees next to me. "I got it. We can prove your father didn't steal it." He set the mask on my lap. "Jax, are you okay? Can you hear me?"

"Tyler," I said.

"Tyler's fine," Ethan told me. "I ran into him on the stairs. He said he'd follow me." Ethan turned around, looking toward the building. "Wait a minute. He was right behind me. Where is he? Oh my God, he's still inside!"

"Jax." Pyrrha clutched my shoulders and shook me. "Why are your eyes closed? Jax, can you hear me?" But I couldn't answer. I fell over on my side.

A siren wailed in the distance.

22

TYLER

Welcome back to the Game.

You are logged in as Tyler. You are seventeen years old. Energy levels are nearly depleted, due to having engaged in hand-to-hand combat with an immortal from the Realm of the Gods. You are also suffering from moderate smoke inhalation and second-degree burns on four fingers. Your adrenal levels are off the chart.

Also, your hair is singed beyond repair. You will require a haircut.

Current status: You have emerged from a burning building, victorious. With the help of your teammates and Hephaestus's flame, you have successfully destroyed the urn of Hope, the urn of Faith, and the urn of Love. Ricardo's followers have been set free.

Your brother, Ethan, and cousin, Jax, are outside the building, awaiting medical attention. Pyrrha, the newest member of your team, is also outside. Congratulations. QUEST COMPLETED.

Game Over.

Pause.

Game Over.

Pause.

Hello? You completed the quest. There is no need to do anything more. You are safe. You are a hero. You should not go back into that burning building. It is too risky. Ricardo is defeated. The Game is over.

Pause.

New Quest Identified.

Objective: Help Pyrrha find her father.

Restart Game.

You are logged in as Tyler. You are seventeen years old and you are not thinking clearly!

23
JAX

Three Months Later

I squirmed in my seat, bored nearly out of my mind. My mom sat next to me. She was dabbing her eyes with a tissue. She was super proud of Tyler. I was proud, too, but I wasn't crying about it. This ceremony felt like forever.

Tyler and his two friends, Walker and the other guy whose name I could never remember, stood on the stage in the Chatham High School auditorium. The mayor of Chatham was giving them the Chatham Youth Brilliance Award. They'd finished their game, Cyclopsville, and it was getting all sorts of attention online. I think they're going to make some serious money. Aunt Cathy said that the first thing Tyler should do with his money is to hire a housecleaning service to decontaminate his room. I agreed with her. Tyler's room smells the worst. According to Ethan, it smells exactly like a Cyclops.

After the whole urn thing was over, and we got back to Chatham, Tyler got real busy with his game, so I got most of the details from Ethan. All about traveling through the portal, and meeting Pandora and Hephaestus. And the Cyclopses. It was really too bad that none of the photos Tyler took had turned out. That would have made the most amazing photo album ever. But Ethan is pretty good with details, so he was able to describe everything they saw and did. Even though I was jealous that I'd missed out, I still liked hearing Ethan tell the story, over and over. In his award speech, Tyler told the audience that he'd met an actual Cyclops and that's how he knew they had yellow blood. Everyone laughed because they thought he was making a joke.

After the fire, I was taken to the hospital. Mom rode in the ambulance with me. She and Uncle

Phil had driven to Philadelphia to find us. Turns out my father, Isaac Romero, had gotten my email. And because he's allowed to make an occasional phone call, he'd called my mom and told her where I was. That's why she and Uncle Phil had raced to Eastern State Penitentiary. During the fire, they'd been stuck out on the sidewalk with all the other people who'd been invited to Ricardo's grand reopening ceremony. But when the urn of Faith was destroyed, all the guards came out of their trances and stopped blocking the gate and the red door. My mom and Uncle Phil ran inside and started looking for us.

I remember a few things about the first day at the hospital. Aunt Cathy had been at a conference, but she arrived only a few hours after me. I got an IV, which was gross because that needle is big and they stick it right into your vein. I also got oxygen and I felt better right away.

Nobody knows this fact, but Tyler went back into the burning building and saved Ricardo. Well, when I say nobody, I mean that the world doesn't know. Only Tyler, Ethan, Pyrrha, Ricardo, and I know the truth. Tyler risked his life for Pyrrha. He's had a huge crush on her since he first saw her in that parking lot outside Merlin's Comics. But he also did it because he's a good person. It didn't matter how evil Ricardo had been, Tyler couldn't ignore the fact that Ricardo was lying on the floor, too weak and confused to escape.

So Tyler went in, and carried Ricardo to safety.

Ethan and I have talked about it a lot and this is what we think happened. When Ricardo opened those urns so long ago, they took hope, faith, and love from him, which explained why he became such a mean, horrid man. Why he left his family. Why he wanted to rule the world. But after the urns were destroyed, Ricardo was overwhelmed by the return of his feelings, and he collapsed. When Tyler brought him out of the fire, Ricardo was weak, barely conscious. But he managed to thank Tyler, and to hug Pyrrha.

And Pyrrha hugged Tyler and told him that she could never repay him for what he did. He'd saved her family. Ethan said she kissed him.

"How did she kiss him?" I asked.

"On the lips."

"Yeah, but what *kind* of a kiss?"

"What do you mean?"

"You know, was it like a little peck, like it didn't

mean anything? Or was it passionate?"

Ethan looked confused. His cheeks got red. "I don't know. It was a kiss. A stupid kiss."

That's how it was with Ethan. If he watched a science experiment, he'd remember every single detail. But a kiss wasn't interesting to him.

We searched online and printed all the newspaper articles about the fire. The cause was officially listed as unknown, but arson was suspected. The popular theory was that one of the cult members set the fire. That's what the newspaper called The New Mount Olympus Corporation—a cult. There was zero mention of any urns. They'd turned to ash. They couldn't hurt anyone ever again.

And all those people who'd been brainwashed, well, they also came out of their trances.

Newspapers reported that the cult leader, Ricardo, had disappeared. There was a warrant for his arrest. And there was a lot to sort out as those ex-followers tried to go back to living normal lives. Some of them had already gotten their money and property back. But for others, it would take time. The museum staff tried to reconnect people with their clothing. I got my purple jacket back. My lucky jacket.

Tyler wasn't the only one who saved someone's father that day. Ethan saved mine. The Mask of Agamemnon that had been sitting on that stage was the same mask that had been stolen from Athens. Police records were reexamined and security footage clearly showed Ricardo walking through the museum before the theft. It took a few months, but my father's arrest was overturned, and he was released. He talked to my mom on the phone. She made me go outside so they could talk in private. I'm not sure what was said, but she cried after the call. She said it was a lot for her to process and we'd discuss it later. I couldn't tell if she was happy or sad. Maybe both.

The Chatham Youth Brilliance Award ceremony was almost over. Tyler finished his speech. I nudged Ethan. We shared a giggle because our great-aunt Juniper had started to snore. She was sitting on the other side of Ethan. Juniper wasn't being rude. She was still healing from her stroke. Her brain was back to normal, but she still needed a cane to walk and she sometimes got sleepy in the middle of the day. The doctor said she'd get her energy back. But she might have the limp for a while. She'd moved in with Mom and me and we were becoming a family again. Ethan and I told Juniper everything that had happened after she'd had her stroke. She was so proud of us for destroying the urns. But we decided it was best not to tell Mom or Uncle Phil or Aunt Cathy. Or anyone else. So Tyler came up with a more believable story.

He said that after coming out of the Museum of Fine Arts in Boston, we drove to Boston Common, to have dinner, but we had some car trouble. Then, while minding our own business, we were taken hostage by Ricardo and driven to Eastern State Penitentiary, where he was going to brainwash us into joining his cult. I managed to send an email to my father, asking for help. But why, our parents asked, didn't I send an email to one of them? Well, that's where Tyler's story goes a bit fuzzy. So when our parents and the police started asking us for more details, we simply acted confused and said we couldn't remember everything. Aunt Cathy has a degree in psychology and she said we all have post-traumatic stress disorder and it might be years before our memories return. If ever. That works for me!

Besides, Tyler's story made so much more sense than the real story. Especially because we had zero proof. The urns were gone. And Pyrrha and Ricardo had taken the leather bag and had returned to their world, where they belonged.

I knew Tyler missed her, but you couldn't tell at that moment. Up on stage, he, Walker, and the other dude bowed. Everyone applauded. Then, after some photos, Tyler joined us outside the auditorium. The trophy was his biggest yet. "We'll have to build a new shelf in the trophy room," Uncle Phil joked. Actually, it wasn't a joke. They had an entire wall for Tyler's trophies.

"We've just met a lady from Microsoft," Tyler told us. "We've got a conference call next week." I have to admit he was looking pretty good for a gamer guy. Aunt Cathy had bought him a suit, and there wasn't a single mustard or ketchup stain on it—yet. And his hair was washed and his face was shaved. If he wanted, he could probably be a model.

Then Tyler turned and his smile got even bigger. We all turned. A girl stood on the far side of the parking lot. You could see her red hair sparkling, even from that far away. "Uh, that's our friend," I told my mom. "We'll be right back." Then Ethan, Tyler, and I ran to Pyrrha.

"Hello," she said. We all hugged her. She carried the leather bag with the golden Poseidon trident. "We departed your world so quickly, I did not have adequate time to thank you."

"Does Zeus know you're here?" Tyler asked worriedly.

"Yes. He has given me permission." She smiled at Tyler. "Hephaestus threatened Zeus. No more thunderbolts or armaments from his forge unless Zeus promised to leave my family alone. Zeus agreed. Thus, my father is reunited with his brother and with my mom. And I am free to travel as I like. What do you think about Disney World?"

"Seriously?" I asked.

"I wouldn't recommend it," Ethan said. "The crowds can get intense, and most of the rides are really loud. Then there are the lines, even for the bathroom. And the germs—"

"It's a blast," Tyler said.

He and Pyrrha were staring at each other and it started to feel weird. "Uh, I think Ethan and I will go wait by the car. See you later," I said.

As we walked away, I turned back. And that's when I saw it. I nudged Ethan and he turned. "See," I told him. "That's what you call a *passionate* kiss."

"Oh," he said. "Noted."

I drove home with my mom and great-aunt Juniper. I sat in the backseat. "Who was that girl?" Mom asked.

"Pandora's daughter," Juniper said with a drowsy voice. Her head rested against the seat and she was starting to fall asleep again. "She's immortal."

Mom glanced at me in the rearview mirror. She gave me a knowing look. "Who is she *really*?"

"She's Tyler girlfriend," I said.

"Oh." Mom smiled. "Well, I'm glad to hear that."

It only took about ten minutes to get home. We drove mostly in silence, so Great-Aunt Juniper could sleep. One of her long white braids hung over the back of the seat. And her red bandana was slipping out of place. I'd fix it when we got home. I liked taking care of her.

A taxi was pulling away from the curb outside our house. A man was standing on the sidewalk. He had one small duffel bag that contained the items that were given to him when he was released from prison. He was waiting for us.

The one purpose, I said to myself as Mom pulled

197

the car into the driveway. Then I threw open the door.

It had taken hope, faith, and love to finish our quest. They were the one purpose.

Acknowledgments

Huge thanks to Annie Anderson, historic site researcher at Eastern State Penitentiary Historic Site, for providing me with maps and photos to help ensure that Jax's journey through the hallways and courtyards was correctly described.

And again, much gratitude to editors Melissa Miller, Claudia Gabel, Katherine Tegen, and the entire team at HarperCollins Publishers. I wrote this novel while trekking through the desert on camel, and my lovely editors never complained about the pages speckled with camel drool, or the envelopes filled with sand.